Strange Star

BOOKS BY EMMA CARROLL

In Darkling Wood

Strange Star

Emma Carroll

Delacorte Press

Text copyright © 2016 by Emma Carroll
Jacket art copyright © 2018 by Anna + Elena Balbusso

All rights reserved. Published in the United States by Delacorte Press, an imprint of Random House Children's Books, a division of Penguin Random House LLC, New York. Originally published in the UK in trade paperback by Faber & Faber Limited, London, in 2016.

Delacorte Press is a registered trademark and the colophon is a trademark of Penguin Random House LLC.

Visit us on the Web! rhcbooks.com

Educators and librarians, for a variety of teaching tools, visit us at RHTeachersLibrarians.com

Library of Congress Cataloging-in-Publication Data
Names: Carroll, Emma, author.
Title: Strange star / Emma Carroll.
Description: First U.S. edition. | New York : Delacorte Press, [2018] | Summary: Told primarily by servant Felix, a former slave, Lord Byron and friends gather to tell ghost stories on a stormy night in 1816 Switzerland, but a scarred girl arrives with her own dark and dangerous tale.
Identifiers: LCCN 2017038517 | ISBN 978-0-399-55605-0 (hc) | ISBN 978-0-399-55606-7 (glb) | ISBN 978-0-399-55607-4 (el)
Subjects: | CYAC: Storytelling—Fiction. | Household employees—Fiction. | Shelley, Mary Wollstonecraft, 1797–1851—Fiction. | Shelley, Percy Bysshe, 1792–1822—Fiction. | Byron, George Gordon Byron, Baron, 1788–1824—Fiction. | Clairmont, Claire, 1798–1879—Fiction. | Supernatural—Fiction. | Adoption—Fiction. | Switzerland—History—19th century—Fiction. | Horror stories. | BISAC: JUVENILE FICTION / Action & Adventure / General. | JUVENILE FICTION / Social Issues / Friendship. | JUVENILE FICTION / Fantasy & Magic.
Classification: LCC PZ7.1.C426 Str 2018 | DDC [Fic]—dc23 LC

The text of this book is set in 11.25-point Amasis.
Interior design by Jaclyn Whalen

Printed in the United States of America
10 9 8 7 6 5 4 3 2 1
First U.S. Edition

Random House Children's Books supports the First Amendment and celebrates the right to read.

For Eliza and Mia

And thou, strange star! ascendant at my birth . . .
—Mary Shelley, "The Choice," 1823

1

A Tale to Freeze the Blood

LAKE GENEVA, SWITZERLAND
JUNE 1816

The company of
Mr. Percy Shelley, Mrs. Mary Shelley,
Miss Claire Clairmont, and Dr. John Polidori
is requested by
Lord Byron
at
the Villa Diodati, Tuesday 18th June, 8 p.m.
Your challenge for the evening is to tell a ghost story
that will terrify the assembled company.

Chapter 1

IT WAS FELIX'S JOB TO deliver the invitation. On such a sparkling, sunny morning after weeks of cold rain he was glad to be outside, stretching his legs. Not that he had far to go—Mr. and Mrs. Shelley's villa was just a short walk through the apple orchard. He'd be back at Diodati again in less than twenty minutes, the job done.

Yet this wasn't just any job. Or any invitation. And despite knowing it was a servant's responsibility to deliver messages, not read them, Felix couldn't resist glancing at the card in his hand. Lord Byron's words, in still-wet ink, read more like a challenge than an invitation. Felix prickled with excitement.

Tonight was going to be spectacular.

Once through the orchard, Felix raced up the steep steps to the Shelleys' front door. His master, Lord Byron, had known Mr. and Mrs. Shelley and Miss Clairmont back in London, where he lived most of the year. Like him, they were writers. Free thinkers—at least, the Shelleys were. Mr. Shelley, a poet, was tall and sickly thin. Mrs. Shelley, smaller, quieter, had the fiercest eyes Felix had ever seen. And Miss Clairmont, stepsister to Mrs. Shelley, was a whirlwind of emotions who cried as much as she laughed. Like Byron, the little group had come here to Switzerland for the summer to take in the mountain air. As individuals, they were interesting enough, but together, their sparks became flames.

At the top of the steps, Felix noticed the shutters at the Shelleys' windows were still closed. It was too early for them to be awake. They'd stayed late at Diodati last night, when, even then, the talk had been strange. They'd spoken of experiments done on corpses. Of a dead frog made to twitch as if alive. It was all Felix could do to trim the candles slowly and pour coffee drip by drip, just to stay in the parlor and listen.

So when he knocked on the front door with a *rat-tat-tat* he didn't expect anyone to answer; the noise simply echoed down the long, empty hallway. The Shelleys didn't care for rules, Lord Byron said. In which case, Felix hoped they wouldn't mind an invitation slipped under the door instead of being delivered safely into their housemaid's hand.

As Felix turned to go he caught a glint of sun on glass. Not every shutter was closed after all. At a small window near the top of the house, someone was watching him. Felix shielded his eyes to get a better look. The person staring down was a child—a girl of about ten—with curls of white-blond hair. Someone—Frau Moritz, probably—had mentioned that the Shelleys had adopted the girl on their travels.

Smiling, Felix raised his hand to wave. "Hullo!" he mouthed.

The girl stared, her eyes as wide as soup plates. Slowly, tentatively, she waved back, though she didn't return his smile.

At the Villa Diodati, Frau Moritz, the housekeeper, was standing on the kitchen steps. The sight of her there, hands on generous hips, made Felix's spirits sink because he knew she was

6

waiting for him. Since Lord Byron's announcement at breakfast of his plans for tonight's gathering, she'd been in a terrible spin. And the person who bore the brunt of it, as ever, was Felix.

"You took your time," she observed.

Frau Moritz liked her household to run as smoothly and precisely as a Swiss clock. Everyone had their place, did their proper work. Even on the outside, the Villa Diodati had that same air of routine. It was a big, square, imposing house with shuttered windows and steep gardens lined with cypress trees. If a house could sit sensibly then Diodati did so in its place on the hillside above the lake named Geneva, after the nearby town. It struck Felix as slightly odd that Lord Byron, with his wild reputation, should spend his summer at such an orderly house. Yet he was a man of many sides, as Felix was quickly learning.

"No more dallying," Frau Moritz said. "We need wood brought in for the fires. Quickly now, my boy."

Nodding, Felix pressed his lips shut. He wasn't *her boy*. Nor was he anyone else's. Those days were disappearing fast, when the color of a person's skin gave them rights over others, his master told him. Apparently, it was the fashion in England for gentlemen to have a black footman. And it was good work too, with smart uniforms and decent pay and a chance to mix with society's finest, which wasn't a thing Felix had thought possible before now.

Frau Moritz had hired him from the marketplace in Geneva, where she'd found him amongst the salamis and pickled vegetables, looking dazed. He'd traveled months and many long miles from America to the French coast, and when his ship docked at Calais, he rode the first cart heading south. He'd never meant to end up somewhere so cold. Frau Moritz's offer of work wasn't charity as such. True, he was skinny and filthy and desperate for a job; truer still was her keen eye for a bargain, since no one round here would pay much for a black servant.

Then Lord Byron arrived for the summer months. He brought with him his doctor, John Polidori, and soon afterwards the Shelleys and Miss Clairmont took lease of the villa next door. Felix had never met people like them. They opened his eyes to a world of possibilities. He began to hope for better. Most of all, he dreamed of his master taking him back to London in the autumn as his footman. And so he set himself a mission this summer, to prove himself worthy of the role.

With his log basket now filled, Felix headed back inside. Climbing the kitchen steps, he felt a sudden twinge in the scar just above his left wrist. The scar was shaped like a ragged letter *S*. Mostly, he kept it hidden under his shirtsleeve in case of questions. Not that he'd run away from America; he'd sailed to Europe a free person and he'd worked hard for that freedom, too.

Yet feeling the twinge stopped him in his tracks. He blinked up at the sky. Pain like this meant a storm was on its way, though currently the morning was still fine. Even the comet that had hung over them these last months was fading so fast it looked no more than a wisp of smoke. From the west a bank of cloud was blooming. The smell of rain was already in the air. Felix shuddered with delight. With a storm as the backdrop, he could only imagine how incredible tonight's ghost stories would sound!

Inside at the kitchen table Frau Moritz's daughter, Agatha, was peeling potatoes. She pretended to ignore Felix; her bowed head with its thick brown plait of hair pinned from ear to ear was all he saw. Still, he felt her eyes slide over him.

8

"Will you tell him, Mama, or shall I?" she called to Frau Moritz, who was at the stove.

"Tell me what?" Felix stopped, resting the log basket on his hip.

Agatha looked up. He glanced between her round, waxy face and Frau Moritz's flushed one.

Wiping her hands on her apron, Frau Moritz joined her daughter at the table. "This gathering tonight of Lord Byron's. It's meant all manner of extra work for us. There's to be a supper for his lordship and his"—she looked disapproving—"*friends.*"

Felix nodded eagerly. "They're telling ghost stories, yes. I'll do the serving, if you like...."

"No, Mama," Agatha cut across. "You promised *me!*"

Felix sucked in his cheeks. He knew what was coming. Just like him, Agatha was fascinated by Lord Byron's friends. Miss Clairmont laughed like a sailor. Mr. Shelley, who looked so deathly pale, was alive with ideas. Even the sullen Dr. Polidori had an interesting, quizzical air. Yet it was Mrs. Shelley who intrigued him most. She seemed so serious and quiet, but when she *did* speak, she was clearly the cleverest of them all. And the way they sat: not upright and polite, but sort of *draped* across the furniture. Felix wanted to breathe these people in, and he sensed Agatha did too.

But Frau Moritz would not choose him to serve over her own flesh and blood. He didn't stand a chance.

Life wasn't fair.

It wasn't fair that in America his mother had worked sugar cane for a white man. Then the white man had branded her newborn baby on the arm with the letter *S,* and said it meant he owned them both.

9

Shifting his log basket onto the other hip, Felix went quickly upstairs. Though not quickly enough, for he heard Frau Moritz say, "Don't fret, Agatha dear. Of course you'll be serving the supper. Lord Byron wants his guests scared by ghost stories, *not* by the servants."

Felix gritted his teeth. It was the type of insult he knew all too well.

Late afternoon the storm arrived. And with it, darkness came early, especially for June. By six o'clock, fires blazed in every room. Special attention was paid to the parlor at the front of the villa, for it was here tonight's ghost stories would be told. The room was grand, with an ornate ceiling and a gleaming wood floor, and four huge windows that looked over the lake. There was little to see by way of a view now, though. Rain had turned the glass into a watery blur.

The fire, at least, looked comforting. As Felix pictured the guests huddled around it to share their stories, his excitement felt almost painful. His disappointment did too. Something marvelous was happening tonight in this house. And he wasn't allowed to attend. Instead, he'd spend his evening miserably belowstairs.

As he made his way back to the kitchens, a sudden thumping at the front door jolted him from his bleak thoughts.

"Ho! Let us in before we perish!"

"Isn't the door unlocked?" someone said, giggling. "Can't we let ourselves in?"

Felix's heart skipped. The guests were early—*two hours* early! It was bound to throw Frau Moritz completely out of kilter. As a servant, he should be flustered too. Yet the Shelleys' obvious disregard for clocks and timings made Felix grin. Hastily, he smoothed his breeches and straightened his jacket. Rushing for the door, he opened it to a peal of thunder, and rain so hard it almost blinded him.

"Goodness! What weather!" cried Miss Clairmont, pushing past to come inside.

The Shelleys followed, sheltering together under an old cape. Though they'd only walked the short distance from next door, their clothes and hair were dark with rain. Mrs. Shelley's boots squelched as she moved.

"I trust you've a good fire for us," Mr. Shelley said as he handed the dripping cape to Felix.

"Yes, sir." He'd carted enough logs inside today to keep them warm until winter. Taking the cape and Miss Clairmont's wet shawl, he shut the front door. The white-haired girl he'd seen earlier at the window wasn't with them, he noticed. But then, ghost stories weren't for children's ears.

"Follow me, if you please," Felix said.

The guests knew their way to the parlor blindfolded. They didn't need a boy in smart breeches to show them. And yet his lordship, for all the rumors, liked certain things done properly. So Felix led the guests down the hallway. Behind him, he sensed Miss Clairmont fretting to get past. She liked bounding into rooms and surprising Lord Byron, who didn't always share her joy.

Rounding the corner, he ran into Frau Moritz.

"Oh, Felix! Whatever's the hurry?" she said.

Then she saw who was behind him. Her frown became a gracious smile.

"Good evening, Herr Shelley, Frau Shelley, Fräulein Clairmont," she said. "Lord Byron and Dr. Polidori await you in

11

the parlor. Do come with me." And to Felix, she hissed, "Tell Agatha she's needed right away."

In the kitchen he found Agatha, mirror in hand, fussing over her hair.

"You're wanted upstairs," Felix said, still irked that she'd been chosen when he worked twice as hard as she ever did.

Agatha looked up, scowling. Then she saw the Shelleys' cloak and Miss Clairmont's shawl, which Felix had hung to dry before the stove. She leapt to her feet, pushing the mirror back into her apron pocket.

"Are they here already?"

"They came early. And like I said, you're wanted."

"But I've not finished preparing supper," she cried, flapping her hands in panic. "How do I look? Am I neat enough?"

Free of its usual plait, Agatha's hair fell in untidy clumps. Her apron front was splattered with tomato pulp. Despite feeling sorely used, a smile crept over Felix's face. *If anyone was going to scare the guests tonight . . .*

"Stop grinning and tell me!" she snapped.

So he pointed out her apron might need changing. She grabbed a fresh one from the drawer, then raced up the stairs just as Frau Moritz came down them in search of her.

By the time Agatha appeared again, supper was ready. Frau Moritz had wiped plates clean and polished the cutlery. But all the chopping and slicing had been Felix's work, and it left him too tired to still be angry. The supper, he had to admit, did look good. There was soft yellow Swiss cheese and a sharp, sour sheep's cheese. Bowls of radishes, pickled nuts, artichokes swimming in oil. There should've been fruit too, but nothing had ripened yet on account of the cold weather. And the bread, dark and coarse, was all they could buy. Still, at least everything was fresh.

"You've remembered Mr. Shelley doesn't eat meat," the housekeeper said with a nod. This was as near to praise as Felix would get.

"Agatha, have the ghost stories started yet?" he asked, once Frau Moritz had finished checking his work.

The girl yawned into her hand. "No. It's really dull. They're talking about the weather—red snow's been falling somewhere or other."

"Red snow?" To Felix this didn't sound dull. Not for a minute.

"It's the comet causing all this queer weather," Frau Moritz said over her shoulder. "Comets are a bad omen. Always have been, always will be."

Yet that didn't explain why it was *still* cold, *still* stormy, even when the comet had nearly disappeared.

The evening grew late. Outside, rain lashed the windows and thunder echoed through the valleys. With the clock on the cabinet showing past ten, Frau Moritz dozed in her seat beside the stove. Nearby, Felix perched on a stool and began to clean his master's shoes, though his heart wasn't in it. He kept thinking of what was happening upstairs.

As if in answer to his question, the kitchen door flew open. Agatha raced down the steps. The clattering of her boot soles woke Frau Moritz with a start.

"Whatever is it, child?" she gasped.

Agatha steadied herself against the table, the color drained from her face.

"I'm not going up there again tonight, so don't ask me." Her voice was shaking: she didn't sound like Agatha at all.

"What's happened?" Felix asked, a delicious, icy feeling worming down his spine.

"Mr. Shelley's just told the most awful tale"—Agatha started to sob—"about a dead person's head being brought back to life."

So the stories had started. And this was just the sort of tale Felix had hoped to hear. He squirmed in horrified delight.

"They want more port wine, but I can't go back up there!" Agatha cried.

Frau Moritz put her arms around her daughter. Over Agatha's head, she caught Felix's eye.

"You want *me* to go up?" he said, in surprise.

"Well, *she* can't go. Look at the lather she's in."

So he put down his cleaning rag and his master's shoes. Finding the port, he hurried from the kitchen before Frau Moritz changed her mind.

Chapter 2

UPSTAIRS, THE PARLOR WAS BARELY recognizable. The room he'd earlier made so comfortable was now as dark as a dungeon. Felix wasn't scared, not like Agatha had been. But he could, as he glanced about him, see her point. The only light came from the fire itself. Shadows stretched up to the ceiling and along the walls. At the windows the shutters remained open, making the huge floor-to-ceiling casements gape like the mouths of caves. It wasn't the slightest bit welcoming. Yet it was the perfect setting for telling ghost stories.

Lord Byron's guests formed an untidy half-circle around the fire. Mrs. Shelley sat on a floor cushion, her feet tucked beneath her. Mr. Shelley, white-faced and uneasy, occupied a chair. Miss Clairmont lay sprawled on the red chaise longue, and next to her, his foot propped on a stool, sat Dr. Polidori. Agatha said the doctor was sweet on Mrs. Shelley and had hurt his ankle jumping from a window to impress her. It was the sort of thing people seemed to do for the Shelleys.

Silently, Felix moved between the guests with the port. Neither Dr. Polidori nor Miss Clairmont looked up as he re-filled their glasses. He was glad they didn't notice how his hand shook.

"Do you have a story for us, Mary?" Dr. Polidori asked, addressing Mrs. Shelley over Felix's shoulder.

"No, sadly," she said. "I'm too exhausted tonight even to think."

Even so, she sat very upright, very tense. If this was exhaustion, then it seemed to be the kind that quivered like catgut pulled tight.

"It's Clara—*again*," said Miss Clairmont, by way of explanation. "That girl is an annoying little wretch. Why Mary and Percy had to adopt her I've no idea. She does nothing but tell lies, then gets into a sulk when no one believes her. She's impossible!"

Felix recalled the girl with white-blond hair he'd seen at the window that morning. So her name was Clara. He didn't think she'd looked sulky; there had been something about her that seemed almost sad.

"I'm sure she'll settle eventually," Mrs. Shelley said, though she didn't sound convinced. "She's tired. It's been a long journey for her—for us all. I left instructions with the maid to put her to bed early tonight."

"Ha! That'll stir up a tantrum," said Miss Clairmont.

Mrs. Shelley glared. "When I want your advice on child-rearing, Claire, do remind me to ask."

"Don't be cruel, Mary dear," said Mr. Shelley as Miss Clairmont winced at the jibe.

Mrs. Shelley turned back to Dr. Polidori. "Forgive me," she said, in softer tones. "I *have* had a trying day, but it's not my daughter's fault. And now my brain feels quite empty of ideas."

Behind those silver-green eyes of hers, Felix felt certain there was nothing *but* ideas. Yet the guests were restless for another ghost story. And so Lord Byron rose from his seat and stood before the fire, elbow resting on the mantel. He cleared his throat dramatically; he did so enjoy *addressing* people.

Felix retreated to the back of the room, eager for the entertainment to resume.

"Who will be our next storyteller? Who will dare to freeze our blood?" His lordship's gaze traveled the group, coming to rest on Mrs. Shelley. "Mary, do you really have no story for us?"

Mrs. Shelley held up her hands in defeat.

"Please, don't ask me again. I cannot think of a single ghostly thing," she said. "Why don't you take my turn?"

Yes, do! Felix pleaded silently, for Lord Byron was brilliant at telling stories. He did voices and actions to enthrall his audience. It was bound to be too good to miss.

"Very well." Lord Byron sighed, as if this were all a huge inconvenience and he'd rather be left alone to sip port. But there was a playful glint in his eye—Felix saw it. His master was enjoying himself.

Moving away from the fireside, Lord Byron took a seat near the windows. Lightning darted across his face, making his skin look a deathly bluish-white. *Almost corpselike,* Felix thought, and felt a churning sensation in his stomach. By the fire the rest of the group had gone very still.

The spell was cast.

"My tale is of a girl named Christabel, who, one dark and stormy night, takes a stranger into her home," Lord Byron said. "That stranger, my dears, is not all she seems."

So Lord Byron began his story, his voice rising and falling like the sea. The way he paused, eyes wide with fear, drew Felix in till he'd quite forgotten himself.

"*. . . Christabel carried the stranger inside, unlocking the huge front gate and staggering across the courtyard. The woman in her arms was so bloodless and weak, she began to wonder if what she'd brought in from the forest was, in fact, a dead . . .*"

Someone cried out.

Felix jumped in alarm. The guests did too, gasping then laughing when they realized it was only Miss Clairmont.

"Don't mock me!" she cried. "I know this tale won't end well, I sense it in my bones."

So did Felix. His heart was already galloping. But taking a deep breath, he told himself not to be foolish. The story wasn't *that* frightening. Yet.

"*. . . As they passed the family dog asleep in its kennel, the animal suddenly awoke. It leapt to its feet, teeth bared white in the moonlight. Christabel was horrified. This dog was known to be as soft as butter. She'd never before heard it so much as growl. Now, though, it snarled at the sleeping form in her arms. Terrified, Christabel hurried indoors.*

"*In the safety of the house . . .*"

A great crash of thunder made his master stop. Felix glanced nervously at the rest of the group. The firelight made their faces look shadowy and hollowed-out, their fear hanging heavy in the air: it was catching. Felix felt his pulse quicken again.

The thunder done, his master took a sip of water, ready to resume. But as he uttered the first word, the drawing-room door opened and a cap-topped head poked around it. Lord Byron's arms fell heavily into his lap.

"What on earth is it, Frau Moritz?" he said, his irritation clear.

Felix groaned inwardly. She'd come looking for him, hadn't she? There was still work to be finished in the kitchens; he'd been up here far too long.

Lord Byron stared at her. "Well? Out with it!"

Frau Moritz shuffled into the room, wringing her hands. "My Agatha's taken a poorly turn. I wondered if the doctor"— she nodded at Polidori—"could come and tell me what to do for her."

She was, Felix realized, not cross but *upset*. It alarmed him.

But Lord Byron was looking thoroughly fed up. It was clear he wasn't concerned for Agatha or Frau Moritz; he wanted only to get on with his story.

He nodded to Felix. "Take him, would you?"

Though badly wanting to stay and hear Christabel's fate, Felix bowed his head. "Very good, my lord."

Down in the kitchen they found Agatha gray-faced and shivering by the stove. An hour earlier, Felix would have got some small satisfaction from the sight of her. Now it unsettled him. Agatha was an irritating, lazy toad of a girl, but she didn't deserve to be scared witless.

"Go back upstairs," Frau Moritz said to him, once he'd settled Dr. Polidori in a nearby chair. "Someone still needs to attend the guests."

Felix was glad to be gone. He didn't like it when people got sick. He'd seen too much of it in his life—in his own family— and he didn't want to think of those memories tonight. As he fumbled his way along the dark hall, he willed his mind to fill up once more with the Christabel story. Was the stranger a villain? A ghost? Would she kill poor Christabel, who in kindness had given her a bed for the night?

He was too late.

On entering the room, he realized the story was over. Lord Byron, slumped in his chair, looked as lifeless as a doll. His master often fasted for days at a time; today was probably such a day. Going to the table where the supper still lay, Felix began putting food on a plate for him.

Miss Clairmont screamed.

Just once—but it went on and on. The plate in Felix's hands trembled violently. He put it down for fear of dropping it and turned to see what was wrong.

"There! At the glass! I saw it!" Miss Clairmont cried. She was pointing at the middle window.

"Saw what?" asked Mr. Shelley.

"A person. All in white. It pressed its hands against the window!"

Mrs. Shelley rolled her eyes. "Is this another of your fancies, Claire?"

Felix glanced at the window. There was nothing to see but darkness and rivulets of rain. Miss Clairmont was crying hysterically now, yet no one seemed to believe her. Lord Byron put his head back and closed his eyes. Mr. and Mrs. Shelley shared a glance.

"Why won't you listen?" Miss Clairmont sobbed.

"Because you're overwrought." Mrs. Shelley put an arm stiffly round her shoulders. "Shall we go to bed? I've still not thought up a story to tell, and you've clearly had quite enough."

The two young women got to their feet. As they made for the door, a noise stopped them dead.

"What's that?" gasped Miss Clairmont.

"A tree tapping against the glass, I suspect," said Mr. Shelley, though he didn't sound sure.

The noise came again, louder this time. A *thud thud thud.* A pause. Then another *thud thud thud,* though it wasn't coming from the window.

Felix knew it exactly. It was the sound a fist made when thumped against wood.

Someone was at the front door.

Chapter 3

"WE MUSTN'T ANSWER IT!" MISS Clairmont cried. "Whoever's out there, don't let them inside!"

Felix looked to Lord Byron, to the Shelleys, hoping someone would tell him what to do. In the story Christabel took a stranger into her home. What became of her in the end? He never got to hear, though he could guess: the group looked terrified.

Thud thud thud.

"I cannot endure that pounding!" Lord Byron said, pressing his fingers to his temples. "Felix, see who it is."

"Yes, my lord." He nodded, determined not to appear scared. This was a chance to prove himself worthy. To show he could keep his head in a crisis and serve his master well. Squaring his shoulders, Felix left the room—this time taking a candle with him.

The knocking went on. Yet bizarrely, the closer he got to the door, the fainter it sounded. Just as he reached for the handle, it stopped completely. Felix hesitated, holding his breath.

Outside, the wind had picked up. There was another flash of lightning. Another thunderclap. Then all fell eerily silent. Felix waited. The knocking didn't resume. A few moments more and he decided whoever had been out there had seen sense and returned home. He breathed again. There was really no need to open the door.

Then came a single *thud*.

Felix jumped. The sound was against the lower part of the door. Someone—or something—was still out there. Bracing himself, he gripped the handle. It wouldn't turn. It felt as if the stupid thing had been greased. Wiping his damp palm on his breeches, he tried again.

A screaming wind blew the door inward so hard it slammed against the wall. The candle died. Everything outside was dark and dripping. There was definitely no one there.

Then he looked down.

In the hall behind him, someone must have opened a door, because a shaft of light spilled onto the doorstep. At his feet was a person. A body. He gasped.

"Oh! Oh my . . ."

Felix's mind leapt backwards. He was on board ship again, sailing from America to Europe with Mother. Those first few days she'd spent mostly on deck. "This is how freedom smells," she'd said.

On the open water the ship was hit by great gray waves that rose from the sea like monsters. The captain ordered everyone to keep below deck. They stayed crammed into the ship's hold for days on end, too many people in bunks awash with vomit and urine. The fever spread fast. Six passengers died in just one night; seven, counting Mother. Their bodies were wrapped in sheets and dropped overboard. He had arrived in Europe alone.

Felix blinked.

He knew a corpse when he saw one, and this girl couldn't

be long dead: only moments ago she'd been knocking at the door. And the body *was* a girl's, he saw, though she wasn't wearing a bonnet, and her frock had seen better days. She lay on her side, knees drawn up. Felix dropped beside her, his hand hovering at her shoulder.

Should I move her? he wondered. *Should I call Lord Byron?*

He wanted to handle things properly, like the best servant of a fine gentleman. And not make a fuss, because there'd already been plenty of that tonight.

Behind him in the hall, someone was approaching. He scrambled to his feet.

"What is it, Felix?" It was Mrs. Shelley. "Is everything all right?"

Stepping aside, he gestured to the girl's body. They both stared in shocked silence.

"Let's bring her inside. We might be able to do something for her," Mrs. Shelley said eventually.

"But she's dead."

Mrs. Shelley shot him a withering look.

"Very good," he muttered.

As Mrs. Shelley put her hands under the girl's arms, Felix took hold of the feet. Together, on the count of three, they lugged her down the hall, a line of filthy water trailing after them.

In the parlor, Mr. Shelley, Lord Byron and Miss Clairmont waited in a nervous huddle.

"Is she dead?" Miss Clairmont cried as they carried the girl in.

"Yes," Felix said.

"We don't yet know." Mrs. Shelley spoke over him.

They laid the girl down on the hearthrug. Gentle though

they were, the movement made her head loll to the side, re-
vealing a strange mark on her neck. It resembled a birthmark
or a visible knot of veins.

"Poor mite," Mr. Shelley remarked, seeing it too. "What an
awful-looking scar."

It was certainly unlike any scar Felix had ever seen. This
one was not the work of a whip or a branding iron—and back
in America he'd had experience of both. The thought made
him tug at his jacket sleeve to make sure the S-shaped mark
on his arm was covered. Then, unsteadily, he got to his feet.

So much for ghost stories.

There'd been no need for tales to freeze the blood. Not
when real life had brought death to the front doorstep. As if,
thought Felix wearily, he needed reminding that the dearest
people, the simplest things could be snatched away in a moment, and only darkness left in their place.

"Our resident doctor should examine her," Lord Byron
said. "Fetch him from the kitchens, Felix. He must've finished
with that servant girl by now."

Felix straightened up.

"Very good," he said.

On his return to the parlor, where a corpse now lay, Dr. Polidori barely flinched. He was used to death, Felix supposed,
though he didn't know how anyone could reach a point where
the sight of a person dead didn't make them feel sad or sick
or . . . something, at least.

"Don't stand there frowning, boy. Out of my way!" Dr. Polidori said. "Now, the rest of you, kindly step back."

The doctor knelt beside the girl. Taking her skinny wrist

between his thumb and forefinger, he watched the mantel clock. Everyone else watched him. Felix had never known a minute to pass so slowly.

Eventually, Dr. Polidori moved aside, rather awkwardly because of his bandaged foot. "I cannot feel a pulse," he declared.

"What about her scar?" Mr. Shelley asked, gesturing to the girl's neck. "It looks almost familiar, though I don't know how."

The mark was now clear to see. It looked dark red and spidery in the firelight. Dr. Polidori leant forward to examine it.

"A disfigurement from birth, most probably," he observed. "I can't imagine it's the cause of death." Which, to Felix's mind, meant he didn't know.

"Oh, right. I see," Mr. Shelley said, moving aside.

With a sudden movement, Mrs. Shelley twisted free of her husband's arms, falling to her knees on the hearthrug. The girl looked more lifeless than ever. Yet, tucking up her skirts, Mrs. Shelley sat directly behind her, wrapping her arms around the girl's waist and heaving her into a sitting position.

"Mary, the girl is dead," Mr. Shelley said, taking hold of his wife's shoulders.

Mrs. Shelley shrugged him off.

"I won't stand back and let her die, not when there's a chance I can help her, Percy. Don't you recall what we witnessed in Somerset?"

Mr. Shelley flinched as if she'd slapped him. Miss Clairmont, who'd been surprisingly quiet until now, gave a low, dreadful moan.

"My nerves cannot bear it," Lord Byron said, clutching his forehead. It was unclear to whom or what he referred, but the playful glint in his eye had now most definitely gone.

The whole mood of the room had changed. It was as if

someone had opened a window and let in the cold; Felix felt the chill of it seeping into his bones. He should do something, he decided. Bring more wine. More firewood and candles.

Then Mrs. Shelley spoke.

"You'll know Percy and I lost our baby girl last year," she said, looking at each of them in turn. "As I grieved, I dreamed I brought her back to life by rubbing her before a fire."

"No, Mary." Mr. Shelley tried to take her arm. She turned away.

"At least let me try," she pleaded. Her eyes, reflecting the firelight, were full of little dancing flames. She looked capable of almost anything.

"It won't work, Mary," Mr. Shelley said. "You're not a scientist. And even if you were . . ." He trailed off dismally.

Just last night they'd spoken of science as a glorious, brilliant thing. Experiments had been done on executed murderers who somehow—in some way—had been revived, or at least made to twitch. More research was needed, of course, but wasn't it exciting? Who knew where all this might lead?

And yet a wave of panic came over Felix, as if he were speeding downhill in a runaway carriage.

You couldn't really bring a person back to life. Could you?

No, he thought, *of course you can't.*

Mrs. Shelley had started rubbing the dead girl's back. Felix shuddered. There was no pleasure in watching, no terrible thrill, but he looked on with a gruesome fascination. In another part of the room, Miss Clairmont was crying again. She demanded to be taken back to their villa. Lord Byron and Mr. Shelley argued over who would accompany her: it seemed both wanted an excuse to leave.

Between the dead girl's shoulder blades, Mrs. Shelley's

hand kept moving. Felix wanted someone to tell her to stop. Though he didn't think anyone could or would. And it made him afraid.

He was aware of the parlor door swishing open. Swishing shut. Lord Byron's voice grew fainter; the others, Felix realized, had gone. His gaze didn't shift from Mrs. Shelley's hand. Round and round it went. On and on and on.

There was sweat on Mrs. Shelley's forehead. Her rubbing wasn't gentle—the tendons in her wrist stood out like cords. That poor girl might have been dough beneath her fist.

And yet, despite himself, he began to feel the smallest tingle of hope.

What if it worked? What if it was actually possible to bring a dead person back to life? Felix stared hard at that hand. As if staring alone would do the trick.

Breathe, he urged the dead girl, *breathe!*

Chapter 4

IT DIDN'T WORK.

The girl's body stayed lifeless. Finally, Mrs. Shelley sat back, exhausted. The only noise was the crackle of the fire, and outside, the storm grumbling around the mountains. Through the windows lightning flickered blue, then white. Heavy with despair, Felix tried to rouse himself to fetch brandy for the shock, a sheet to cover the body. But he'd fallen into a sort of trance.

How mad to think a dead girl could be brought back to life! What on earth were those scientists thinking of, making people hope like that, making Mrs. Shelley believe? For a moment there, he'd almost fallen for it himself.

"Let's lay her on the chaise longue," Mrs. Shelley said.

"Yes, Mrs. Shelley."

"For heaven's sake, stop calling me Mrs. Shelley!"

Felix blinked. He was the servant—he *always* called her by her proper title.

"Don't look so put out," she muttered. "Percy and I are not married. So really I'm Miss Godwin. Mary Godwin."

"But on the invitation it said Mrs. Shelley."

"That's just for appearances."

"Oh." He was still confused. So the Shelleys weren't

29

husband and wife, but two people who lived together and had children. He'd not realized people did that. So many rules were being broken tonight, he was struggling to keep up.

"Please, call me Mary," she said.

"Mary." Felix nodded. It sounded daring, and he liked it.

Together they lifted the girl onto the chaise longue. In the candlelight, she looked about fourteen, he guessed. Her eyelashes were startlingly long, and she'd a sprinkle of freckles across her nose. It was a nice face, the sort that would be missed, and it vaguely reminded him of someone.

"Shouldn't we fold her arms over her chest?" Felix asked, because that was what he'd done when Mother died.

"Would you do it?" Mary said. "I don't think I can touch her again."

"Very well."

Lifting her right arm, Felix laid it across her body, then did the same with her left. The muscles hadn't yet set. Nor had her skin cooled, which he supposed was due to heat from the fire. She still wore a pair of clogs that had rubbed her heels raw. He slipped them off gently, and seeing her toes so grimy with dirt made him sad.

"I'm going to fetch water to wash her feet." Then he saw the look on Mary's face. "What's wrong?"

Mary pressed her hands to her mouth.

"My goodness. I think I know her!" Forgetting her desire not to touch, Mary reached forward to smooth the girl's hair from her neck. In doing so, she again revealed the scar. "I'm sure it is . . . I know that mark . . . and yet it's hardly possible she should come all this way!"

All this way?

So the girl wasn't local, then. This much Felix understood,

for she wasn't dark like the Italians or flaxen-haired like the Swiss, and both lived up here in the mountains. No, this girl was as freckled as a hen's egg. Yet still she felt familiar, somehow.

"Why would she come here?" Felix asked.

Mary didn't answer. Her mouth fell open.

"Goodness!" she cried. "Look!"

The girl's arms had dropped to her sides. Felix frowned. Now he'd have to arrange her all over again, and he wasn't sure he wanted to, not when she felt so unexpectedly warm.

Then he realized. Something was happening.

The girl's feet twitched. The lump in her throat bobbed up and down. Her eyelids trembled, then opened. Felix felt his own jaw drop. Mary cried out, sinking to her knees to take the girl's hand.

"She's alive!" Mary cried. "Felix, look! She's alive!"

Felix *was* looking. Not just at the poor dazed girl, but at Mary herself. It made him catch his breath.

"We saved her," Mary said.

Tears ran down her cheeks. She was thinking of her baby, Felix thought, whom she'd lost, then dreamed of warming by the fire. In the confusion of feelings that tore through him, his eyes misted over. There would always be those who couldn't be saved.

The girl revived quickly, though she was very weak; she'd clearly not eaten for days. Once they'd propped her up against cushions and tucked a blanket over her legs, Felix warmed brandy and milk at the hearth.

"Ta very much." Speaking huskily after she'd downed the

31

drink, the girl held out her cup for Felix to refill. This time she gulped greedily.

"Slow down!" Mary said. "Or you'll be sick."

On hearing Mary's voice, the girl froze. Very slowly, she lowered the cup from her mouth. A line of milk clung to her top lip, yet she looked deadly serious.

"I found you, miss," she said.

Outside, the thunder grew loud again. A fresh squall of rain rattled the windows, making the room feel darker and colder.

Mary peered closely at the girl. "I *do* know you, don't I?"

"You do, miss. You know my sister too," she said, growing agitated. "I've come all this way to find her. It's taken me weeks, but I'm here now, and if you've so much as harmed a hair on her head, I'll—"

"What *is* this nonsense?" Mary interrupted. "For goodness' sake, calm yourself, child!"

Felix was confused. So Mary really did know the visitor. And the girl just mentioned a *sister*?

The girl wiped her mouth with the back of her hand. She looked nervous, unable to meet Mary's gaze. "You came to Somersetshire in England, miss, to a place called Eden Court, you'll remember?"

As she talked, Felix heard the strangeness in her voice, the "r" sound lingering on her tongue. He didn't know these places she spoke of, but Mary obviously did, for she stiffened.

"Of course!" Mary said a bit too brightly. "We visited Eden Court a few weeks ago, before we left for Switzerland. Francesca Stine is an old friend. There are so few women scientists in practice. She's quite incredible. So many ideas! Such a brilliant mind!"

The girl recoiled. "That's not all she is."

"Yes, I remember you being there," Mary said, as if she

hadn't heard. "It was the night of that big storm, wasn't it? We had to leave suddenly because—"

"Your father came looking for you, miss." Now it was the girl's turn to interrupt. "And I was mighty glad he did, let me tell you."

Mary's smile faded. "I don't believe we need speak of that now."

"Maybe not of that, miss," the girl said. She'd grown pale again. Her fingers fidgeted against the sides of the cup. "But there's plenty else that needs saying concerning my sister. Please, tell me she's safe."

Felix frowned: this was getting more intriguing by the minute.

Mary seemed confused too. "I don't understand. At Eden Court, you were a servant, weren't you?"

"Not exactly, no."

She didn't look like a servant, not to Felix. She wasn't coarse-featured like Agatha. Her hands weren't chapped either, but her nails were dirty, and her arms, though thin, looked strong. Her frock was a size or two too big. And those clogs that didn't fit might once have belonged to someone else.

"My name is Lizzie Appleby," the girl said, taking a long, nervous breath. "I live in Sweepfield, the village near to Eden Court, and . . ." Her voice trembled. "I had to come after you! I couldn't bear to think of what you might do!"

"But how did you find us?"

"That night at Eden Court you were talking amongst yourselves, of this place called Diodati. I remembered the name—I don't reckon I'll ever forget it."

A great flash of lightning silenced her. The girl called Lizzie buried her face in her arms. She seemed suddenly terrified.

Felix shuffled his feet. He wanted to help but didn't know how. In the end he crossed to the table, piling bread and meat onto a plate. He didn't suppose Lizzie Appleby would eat much with her head in her arms. But at least he could try.

Once the thunder and lightning passed, she lifted her head and wiped her face with her hands.

"Here, Lizzie." Felix offered her the plate of food. She didn't take it, so he placed it gently in her lap. She looked up. Just once. Then her gaze slid away again. He wondered if there was something wrong with her eyes.

"I'm sorry," Lizzie said. "'Tis the lightning. It scares me so."

His gaze flickered briefly over the blemish on her neck. Again, he wondered how she'd got the strange mark. But he knew better than to ask; scars sometimes meant there was a story too private and painful to share.

Mary cleared her throat. "Now, what's this about a sister?"

"*My* sister, miss. She's mine. And you took her against her will."

Felix stared, appalled.

"What do you mean? I did no such thing!" Mary said indignantly.

"What makes you think she's here with Mary?" Felix asked.

"I took no one without permission," Mary said.

Felix glanced at her. She looked like she always did: cool. Thoughtful. Only this time her jaw was set tight.

"I was told she was an orphan, with nowhere to go—I thought we were being kind. . . ."

"*Kind?*" Lizzie laughed in disbelief.

Mary breathed deeply again. A red flush was creeping up her throat.

"Felix! Do stop hovering and sit," she snapped.

But he'd never sat in a room abovestairs before. This was another rule about to crumble to dust. "Sit *where?*"

Mary clicked her fingers at a nearby chair. Awkward though it was, Felix did as he was bid, and prayed Frau Moritz wouldn't walk in and see.

"This sister you speak of," Mary said, her composure regained. "I was told she had no proper relatives. No one cared for her. The locals had shunned her."

"Who told you this?" Lizzie asked.

"Why, Miss Stine, and the girl herself."

"My sister doesn't always tell the honest truth, miss."

Mary blinked. "Well, I believed her. She was distraught. She needed a fresh start away from Sweepfield. I'll admit she took some persuading to come with us at first, but she's seen sense now and we're happy together—"

"So she's safe?" Lizzie cut in. "She's all right?"

"Of course she's all right! Why wouldn't she be?" Mary said irritably. And yet Felix saw the relief on Lizzie's face. "If this is a case of your word against mine, then your journey has been wasted."

There was a long, tense, fidgety silence. It was Lizzie who broke it. "To decide that, you'll need to *hear* my word."

Mary twitched uneasily. "Very well."

"Felix?" Lizzie asked. "Will you listen too?"

"Yes . . . yes, all right." He was taken aback to be included, and decided he rather liked her for it.

She gave a nod of thanks. Yet she still didn't look at either of them, staring instead at the plate of food in her lap.

"Eden Court is not all you think it to be," Lizzie explained. "That night you came, I wasn't a servant. I was a prisoner."

Mary gave a gasp. Felix sat forward in his seat.

35

"What went on in that house wasn't wonderful or"—Lizzie took a shaky breath—"exciting. It was proper awful. I need to tell you everything, miss, and quickly, because I've a suspicion someone else is on their way here too, someone I don't ever wish to meet again."

Felix glanced at the windows with their shutters still open. This mysterious *someone* might be out there right now.

"I'll bolt the front door," he said.

On returning, Felix closed the shutters. Not seeing those huge dark windows helped a little, though his heart still beat surprisingly fast.

"I beg that you'll believe me—both of you," Lizzie pleaded.

Felix nodded in earnest. Her filthy skirt hems and poor, raw feet spoke of the miles she'd traveled to be here. Of the mountains she'd crossed and sea she'd sailed. It took courage to do so. It also took fear. However bad the journey, it was better than what was left behind.

Felix knew how that felt.

Something terrible had happened to Lizzie Appleby, and whatever she was about to tell them, a big part of him already believed her.

2

Lizzie's Tale

SWEEPFIELD, SOMERSETSHIRE

DECEMBER 1815–MAY 1816

Chapter 5

CHANGE WAS COMING. YOU COULD smell it in the air, all sharp
and peppery like radishes. Even our little village of Sweepfield felt restless. Every week brought talk of new discoveries:
a lamp lit by electricity, a steam-powered engine, a needle that
went in your arm to stop the pox. Down in the valleys, villages
grew into towns, and towns grew into cities, getting bigger and
busier by the day. One morning we'd wake up and find Bristol
on our doorstep, folks said. These were uneasy, exciting times.

There was one night, though, when the Old Ways won out.
And that was Midwinter's Eve in Pilgrim's Meadow around
the bonfire. We gathered to celebrate the end of the year with
feasting and music and stomping, swirling dances. It was a
time for feeling glad to be alive. For on Midwinter's Eve, the
spirit world came close to ours—so close, some said, you'd
see the ghosts of those soon to be dead.

I'd grown up with these superstitions running through my
bones. They were part of Midwinter's Eve. Part of the thrill.
Yet this year felt different, and all because of a strange sort of
star in the sky.

The night of the festival was cold and full of starlight. One
in particular shone brighter than the rest. It had a tail too, which

made it look like a very bright tadpole. It had first appeared a week before. "That isn't a star, Lizzie, that's a comet. It's a different thing entirely," Mam had said when we'd been rounding up our geese for the night and I spotted it in the sky. "Old lore has it that they bring plague and famine and terrible fortune." She said it all wide-eyed and splayed-fingered, with laughter in her voice. And I laughed back, or pretended to.

Tonight the comet had grown larger. It sat low and heavy in the sky and felt like a nagging inside my head—of what, I didn't know. We were here to celebrate Midwinter's Eve, as our ancestors had done before us. It was a time for fun, and for stamping your feet against the cold, *not* for staring moodily at comets. All down one side of Pilgrim's Meadow were food stalls selling roast pork, meat pies, hot currant buns. Potatoes baked in a pit dug into the ground. There was a cider stall, spiced wine, a tethered Jersey cow whose milk cost a penny a cup or nothing if you milked her yourself.

Right in the middle of the field, we'd built the bonfire. It was as tall as a house and as wide as a ship, and now the whole of Sweepfield village—all two hundred and twelve souls—stood around it, their faces glowing yellow in the firelight. It meant that whilst your back parts froze, your front sweated in the heat. My friend Mercy Matthews insisted we keep our distance from the flames.

"Otherwise my face'll go awful blotchy," she said.

I'd never seen Mercy look *remotely* blotchy. She had inky dark hair that fell below her waist and eyes the color of blackbirds' eggs. Even now, freezing and miserable, her nose was a lovely frost-nipped pink. She was, by far, the prettiest girl in Sweepfield and beyond. Everyone but Mercy herself knew it.

Moving back from the fire didn't restore her spirits. It simply made us grow colder. My nine-year-old sister, Peg, tried waving a bag of licorice in Mercy's direction; that didn't work either.

"I can't eat," she said glumly.

Peg looked at Mercy, then at me as I raised my eyebrows. Mercy refusing sweets was like a fish refusing water. But I guessed what—or rather *who*—the matter was. Only one person had this effect on Mercy: Isaac Blake.

"Come now, cheer up!" I tried giving her a playful nudge. But the Old Ways also had it that Midwinter's Eve was a time to discover true love, and it was this, I suspected, that was making Mercy so quiet.

Part of me understood how she felt. Not the true love thing—blimey, no. The boys in our village were a grubby-faced, gangly-limbed bunch, yet still thought themselves to be princes. That included Isaac Blake, the lad Mercy was soft on, and who, in my view, was not good enough to clean her boots. Like Mercy, though, I didn't feel quite myself tonight, but I was determined to shake it off.

Slipping my arm through Mercy's, I tried to be cheery for us both. "So, what exciting things have been happening in Sweepfield today? Any murders? Any grave-robbing? Anyone's horse cast a shoe?"—the latter being the most likely.

Mercy shrugged. Her mam ran the village bakery, where people without ovens took their bread and pies for cooking, or bought from her instead. She knew everyone's business. A person only had to pick their nose and we'd heard about it by midday.

"I suppose you know about the scientist?" she said.

41

Strangely, I didn't. "Eh? What scientist?"

"He's moving down from London, it seems, and renting Eden Court for the year."

"That's a big house for one person to live in, isn't it?" chipped in Peg.

She was right. Eden Court was a tall, gray, forbidding place with turrets and battlements that made it seem like a castle. It sat two miles west of our village, where its jagged roofline was just visible from the road. A very rich, slightly mad family had once lived there. Nowadays it stood empty. The driveway was choked with weeds and the gates were always locked.

"Can't think why anyone would want to live there," I said. "It gives me the shivers."

"Well, he's hired servants to make it nice again. They've been scrubbing floors like mad and airing out all the rooms, to make the place ready for when he arrives," Mercy said, then added, "So I've heard," which meant her mam had told her, so it was bound to be true.

I caught sight of my own mam then. She stood nearer the fire than we did. It was easy to pick her out in the crowd. No other grown-up had hair like hers—a mass of pale blond curls that stood out from her head. Peg's hair was the same. And in the glow of the bonfire, it blazed with light.

Like a comet's tail.

The thought unnerved me: it didn't seem right to link Mam with that ominous-looking thing in the sky. So I was glad when Mercy talked of prettiness instead. For that was what Mam was—pretty—though it wasn't all that she was—far from it.

"Your mam's proper handsome, in't she?" Mercy sighed. "She in't plain-faced like all the other mams. She's got a real magic about her."

42

"Don't let her hear you saying that," I said, though I was a little bit pleased.

It was what you *did* that mattered, Mam always claimed. She didn't hold much stock with magic and superstitions. While Da was in his workshop making chairs and cabinets, Mam tended the house and our animals. Peg and me had to help out too; so did Da when the need arose. But it was Mam who worked hardest and fastest. It was a job to even try to keep up.

Tonight, she'd woven white winter roses into her and Peg's hair. She tried to do mine but they wouldn't stay, my hair being too straight and slippery. Reaching out, I pushed a stray flower back into Peg's curls.

"Are the other ones all right?" said Peg, letting go of my hand to pat her head.

I did a quick check. "They're fine."

It was then I happened to glance down at her frock, and saw something wriggling inside her pocket.

"Oh, Peg," I groaned. "What've you got in there this time?"

Last week, she'd brought home a shrew. Before that, she had a slowworm. And before that, a hedgehog, which escaped and hid under the log pile. These pets of hers were becoming a habit.

"It's a little field mouse. I've called him Acorn. They were moving that hayrick in the top field and I saved him from getting stamped on," Peg said.

Now, I knew for a fact they had moved the hayrick back in September, so this was one of Peg's little white lies. Not a big, bad lie, just a not-quite-truth, spoken in such a sweet way that folks didn't think to doubt her.

"Look at him, Lizzie. He's such a dear," Peg said.

A tiny fawn head popped out of her pocket. Mercy screwed her nose up in disgust. "Ugh! And in the same pocket as the licorice too!"

I couldn't help but laugh. "Well, it isn't coming into our bed this time. Not after that shrew got inside my pillowcase."

"Acorn's going to live outside," Peg said. "Promise he is."

One look at her huge brown eyes and I doubted it, somehow, not in this weather. It was toe-numbingly cold. And there was no better way to warm up than a spot of dancing, I decided. By now I'd had enough of big-sistering Peg.

"Come on, let's find Da," I said to her. "It's time he took you home, anyhow."

We found him at the cider stall in the midst of a rowdy crowd. On seeing us, Da put an arm round Peg's shoulders and smiled glassily: he'd had more to drink than usual. It didn't make him louder, though; if anything, he looked gentler, more dreamy-faced.

"Time for bed, poppet?" he asked Peg, who grumbled a bit. Then to me: "Two dances, Lizzie love, then home, all right?"

In a far corner of the field came the sound of fiddles starting up. Drumbeats wafted towards us on the icy breeze. Mercy caught my eye. We grinned like idiots at each other.

"All right, Da," I said. "Two dances. I promise."

Chapter 6

WE RAN TOWARDS THE MUSIC, tripping and giggling over the frosty grass. Reaching the far side of the field, we slowed to a walk to get our breath back.

"Oh, Mercy!" I squealed. "Look!"

A square had been marked out for dancing. In each corner a flaming torch burned, and there were hay bales for sitting on, most of which were already occupied. No one was dancing yet, but that square of ice-white grass looked so inviting, it made my insides tremble. For the first time all evening, I felt my spirits truly lift. I'd no idea how I'd keep to my promise of just two dances. Mercy, though, had turned glum again.

"I hope Isaac isn't here," she said.

I rolled my eyes. This Isaac Blake business had turned her into something of a sop. "Have you two had cross words?"

"Might've," she said, flicking her hair over her shoulder. "We were meant to go walking today but he said he had a sick pig to tend. Honestly, Lizzie, he cares more for those animals than he ever does for me. So if he asks me to dance tonight, I shan't."

I glanced at her sideways. *Good,* I thought. It was time she realized boys like Isaac Blake weren't a catch. She was better off without him.

At the edge of the dancing space, people had started jostling and cheering. We stood on tiptoe to get a look. With a sudden roar, the crowd parted. Cheers went up as a boy, his eyes covered in a red scarf, stumbled into the square.

"Oh!" I cried, clapping my hands in delight. "It's the blindfold game!"

It was an old Midwinter's Eve tradition. Whoever the blindfolded person touched then became their true love. Last year, Miss Parks the postmistress touched the arm of Mr. Henderson, who owned the biggest farm in Sweepfield. Mam had sworn it was an accident, that Miss Parks had just slipped in the mud. Yet sure enough, the two were married by Easter.

Amidst whooping and whistling, the blindfolded boy did an unsteady lap of the crowd. His big flappy feet looked familiar somehow. So did his tufty brown hair. Mercy clearly thought the same.

"It's Isaac!" Mercy gripped my arm. "Let's get closer! Quick!"

I frowned. "Hold on, I thought you said . . ."

But she was already elbowing her way down to the front, dragging me with her.

"Isaac!" Mercy cried, positioning herself right in his path.

The cheering got louder. Faster. Isaac came back in our direction again. Mercy stretched out her arm.

"Over here!" she cried, waving madly. "Isaac! It's me!"

There was no telling whether he could hear her. There was too much whooping. Too much shouting. Whipped up in the excitement, I became part of it, yelling till my throat hurt. Isaac came closer—close enough for me to see the dirt under his fingernails. Mercy leaned as far forward as she could, until their hands were just inches apart. Then, right at the last, he turned away. The crowd let out a mighty "Ohhhh!"

"Go to *him*!" I said, nudging Mercy, for by now I suspected he knew it was her and was playing up on purpose.

All of a sudden, Isaac stopped. He reached out again in our direction. Oh crikey! In *my* direction! Though I twisted away, he somehow got hold of me.

"Get off, you great idiot!" I hissed.

Instead, he lifted my arm above his head like a prize. A massive, roaring cheer went up, making me want to die on the spot. I hardly dared look at Mercy, who I could feel was staring daggers at me. I tried to escape Isaac's grasp, but he held on tight. And with his free hand he pulled down his blindfold to gawp at me like the half-wit he was.

"Lizzie Appleby?" he said. "It can't be true."

"No," I said. "It honestly *can't* be." Flustered, I tried to make Mercy swap places with me.

"Stop it!" she cried.

Shaking me off, she ducked through the crowd. Isaac let go of me. I rushed after my friend—my *best* friend. "Mercy! Wait a minute!"

Isaac called out too. "Awww, come now, Mercy! Don't take on. I was only joking."

Our cries fell on deaf ears. Without a backwards glance, Mercy struck out across the field.

"It's only a game, Mercy!" I yelled.

She was heading for the field gate; I could just about see the pale gray of her shawl glowing in the darkness. Behind me, Isaac's voice grew fainter and crosser. "Don't listen, then. See if I care, Mercy Matthews."

Mercy didn't stop. Once through the gate, she went straight down the lane to the churchyard, which was the quickest route home. I lost sight of her after that. And by the time I reached the field gate, I felt proper dismal. Mercy didn't truly think I liked Isaac, did she? It was only a silly village tradition.

Up ahead, the church clock chimed midnight. I didn't fancy taking the shortcut through the churchyard with only the light of the comet to guide me. The trees overhead were stark and bare, their shadows as spindly as a dead woman's fingers. So I took the long way home, through the center of Sweepfield, past the village green. Lost in my sorrows, I didn't hear footsteps behind me. A hand fell heavy on my shoulder. I spun round so fast, my heart stopped.

"Shhhh! It's me! Don't scream!"

Mercy stood before me. I half gasped, half laughed with relief.

"We mustn't quarrel over that stupid boy. . . ." I stopped.

Mercy wasn't angry, I realized. Her face had gone as pale as her shawl. A chill passed right through me.

"Whatever's the matter?" I said.

She took both my hands. Her fingers were freezing. "I've just seen something awful in the churchyard."

"What, Isaac Blake?"

She didn't laugh. Nor did I.

"I saw your mam, Lizzie. And I think I saw you too."

I snatched my hands from hers.

"That's a mean trick to play," I said. "Are you getting back at me over Isaac?"

"No!"

Something in her look made me believe her. I knew the superstition as well as she did: Pass by a church at midnight on Midwinter's Eve and you'd see entering it the souls of those who'd face death within the year. Those who came out again would survive. And those who didn't . . .

"It's a meaningless tradition," I said quickly. "Just like that blindfold game. You mustn't believe it, because it doesn't stand for anything. Anyway, Mam and me—we both came out again, didn't we?"

Mercy put a hand over her mouth. "Oh, Lizzie," she said, and started to cry.

Chapter 7

YOU ONLY HAD TO LOOK at Mam to see she was as strong as a bull. Anyone with any sense knew that Mercy's vision was just an old myth, as daft as that game that had me and Isaac Blake paired for life. The best thing I could do was to forget about it. And for a while, I almost did.

As the old year died and 1816 arrived, it brought the most dismal weather I'd ever known. Rain fell for weeks on end. It blew down our chimney, leaked through our thatched roof, and made each walk to the field to feed the livestock like swimming in a river of brown soup. As usual, Sweepfield folks were keen to find something to blame. Everything of late had been the fault of the comet, and so was the case with our weather.

One soggy February morning, we were in our kitchen about to eat. We'd already been out to feed the pigs in our orchard, and our wet boots and stockings hung steaming before the fire. The work wasn't over yet, though. There were still the cattle that grazed land further down Crockers Lane. As it was such a job to feed them in this weather, Da had promised to help.

"Breakfast first," Mam insisted.

She cooked oatmeal in our smallest pan: the other, bigger

ones sat on the floor beneath a particularly leaky bit of ceiling, catching rainwater drips. As she was dishing up, someone knocked hard at the front door. Mam's ladle hovered over my bowl.

"Who on earth can that be?" she said.

Only strangers ever used our front door. It opened straight onto Crockers Lane, which Da said made it dangerous because the road was often busy with carters who drove their horses too fast. We used the kitchen door that led into our backyard, and so did any villagers who called.

"I'll go," said Da. Getting to his feet, he gave me and Peg a pretend-serious glare. "No touching my food, you pair of greedy guts."

He needn't have worried. We were far more interested in who was on our front step, and crept to the doorway to eavesdrop.

The caller, we discovered, was a manservant from Eden Court, the big house two miles hence. Mercy had said a scientist was moving in there, and so, in the hope of more tidbits of information, I listened especially hard.

"You see, Mr. Appleby, our tenant from London is arriving any day," the manservant said. "Yet in opening up one of the downstairs rooms, we've found the shelving is ruined with damp."

"Damp'll do the trick," Da agreed.

"As you're a carpenter, Mr. Appleby, can you replace it?" said the man, in agitated tones. "And quickly too? The new tenant has much"—he paused—"equipment. Not being able to store it properly will be holding up important work."

The manservant didn't say the new tenant was a scientist, but it was obvious this was what he meant. The "important work" part sounded intriguing. I couldn't wait to tell Mercy all about it.

"I see," said Da.

"We need you to come to the house this morning to take measurements, if you please. We're desperate to get this finished before our tenant arrives."

On the spot, Da said he could do it.

Back at the kitchen table, Mam scraped her bowl so hard it made a screeching noise. "You've forgotten the cattle, have you?" she said to Da. "Are we to carry all that feed by ourselves?"

Da sighed gently; he didn't like arguing, especially not with Mam, who was good at it.

"You could wait an hour or two, my love," he said. "Just until I've been to Eden Court and measured where they're wanting these shelves put."

Mam gestured towards the window. "But the rain's actually stopped out there. Another couple of hours and it'll be at it again."

The wind had changed too, I'd noticed. It no longer blew mild and gusty down the chimney but seeped icily under the back door. What fell from the sky next might well be snow. And that would make reaching the cattle even harder.

"We need this Eden Court job, Sarah. It's important I go," Da said, and his face was so lit with excitement, I wanted to smile.

The look Mam gave him, though, was deadly. I almost laughed, but it came out as a cough. Peg passed me her cup of water.

"'Tis *important* our cattle survive the winter and all," Mam said. "What's so urgent about a set of shelves, anyway?"

"Mercy says the new tenant is a scientist," I said, hoping to lighten the mood.

Mam rolled her eyes. "Oh, and isn't that just what we need round here—a rich man with chemicals who thinks he can change the world!"

Pushing back his chair, Da got to his feet. He'd not even touched his oatmeal.

"I'll be in my workshop," he said. The back door slammed shut behind him.

Mam pulled a face. "Well," she said, slapping her hands down on the table.

She wasn't happy, that much was obvious, and yet still I felt a pang of pride for our da. It was quite something that Eden Court wanted his carpentry skills. Anyway, it was stupid to keep lugging feed up Crockers Lane in this weather.

"We should've kept the cattle close to the house. It would've made things a fat lot easier," I said.

"But the orchard's got our pigs in it," said Peg.

"Not for much longer," I reminded her.

Peg covered her ears. "Don't talk about the butchers. You know I hate it when they go for meat."

Mam, though, seized on what I'd said. "By heck, Lizzie, you're right. Actually, we still *could* bring the cattle down here. The grass is so poor they're eating hay anyway. It won't matter if we put them in with the pigs for a few days." And she beamed at me as if I were suddenly the cleverest, most wonderful person in the world. "Tell you what, shall we do it now?"

My mouth dropped. "The whole lot? *Now?* Without Da? But there's twelve of them and they're awful skittish."

"Nonsense! We'll get them down here quicker than your da can even *think* Eden Court shelves. We don't really need his help for this."

I gawped at her. So my mam reckoned we could herd twelve longhorn cattle down Crockers Lane. That meant rounding them up, getting them out the gate and through a sea of mud, all the way to our orchard. And before the weather set in again. She was, without question, insane.

Seeing my face, Mam laughed.

"Lizzie, my love," she said, touching my cheek. "Don't doubt what you're capable of."

Her hand felt warm against my skin. She was smiling at me, *for* me. And in that moment I believed her. Once the weather turned, it'd be harder than ever to feed the cattle. Before I knew it, I'd agreed: yes, we'd bring the cattle down to our orchard. We even spat on our palms and shook hands to seal the deal.

Peg and me gulped down the rest of our oatmeal: we had to, with Mam stood over us, toe tapping on the flagstones. She'd noticed too how the wind had changed, and kept glancing out the window at the sky.

Once we'd clothed ourselves in shawls and almost-dry boots, Mam hurried us across the yard. The door to Da's workshop stood half open; through it I glimpsed him sorting his tools, and again felt that surge of pride.

"Don't bother your father; he's busy," Mam said.

"Shouldn't we tell him what we're doing?"

"He'll see soon enough. Now stop dithering." Grabbing my arm, she tugged me onwards. It was typical Mam, letting her actions speak louder than words. But it made me nervous. I didn't like lies; they had a way of catching you out.

Chapter 8

OUR FIELD WAS A FOURTEEN-ACRE spot that ran uphill as far as the churchyard wall. By the time we reached it, our feet and skirt hems were soaked again. We were out of breath too. In the cold air, the mud on Crockers Lane had turned thicker, making the walk slow and tiring. On the smaller puddles, ice had already begun to form, and the sky had that strange, swollen look that signaled snow was on its way.

Once inside the gate, Mam cupped her hands to her mouth. Her holler brought twelve hungry longhorn cattle lumbering down the hill towards us. They were expecting hay and turnips, so the sight of us empty-handed brought them to a slithering halt about thirty yards away.

Mam called again. They watched us warily. One beast took a step forward, then stopped and blew steam through his nose. The rest simply stood, staring.

"What do we do now?" I said.

"I'll go round the back of them," said Mam. "You stay by the gate."

It wasn't that simple.

One step towards them and the cattle took off in a whirl of hooves and mud. When they reached the far wall they stopped again, their great freckled heads bent low. It was then I noticed how the light had changed. The grass, the hedge, the cattle all looked leached of color. A blast of wind blew my wet skirts tight against my legs, and I felt the first snowflakes tickle my face.

"The weather's turned." I glanced worriedly at the sky.

"All the more reason to bring them in today," said Mam. She'd brought with her a pitchfork for nudging the cattle's rumps; she pointed it now at us. "Don't move. Either of you."

As Mam strode off across the field, Peg began to grizzle. "I'm cold, Lizzie. Can't we go home?"

"Soon, I promise."

Narrowing my eyes, I watched as Mam walked a wide arc around the cattle, her arms held open. The beasts stayed very still, allowing her to get close. Then, in a finger snap, they leapt away. Some went left, some went right, the ground thudding with their hoofbeats. When finally they did stop, they stood wide-eyed and nervous, scattered across the field.

Peg frowned. "They aren't behaving, are they?"

They weren't. Nor was the weather. The sky had gone a sickly shade—a sort of gray tinged with yellow. Snow fell faster now. Little hard grains of it whipped and spun before my eyes. At our feet, the grass was turning white.

Mam came striding back across the field, red-cheeked and irritable. "Right, girls, listen to me: this isn't working. We need to try another way."

The wind blew so hard it was a job to even hear her. Then came another noise, so unexpected I didn't think it real. It rumbled above our heads like an animal growling, or something heavy dragged across a flagstone floor.

Peg's mouth turned down at the corners. "I don't like it, Lizzie," she wailed.

"Don't fret. 'Tis only thunder," I said.

But I didn't like it either, not after what folks in the village had been saying about this freakish weather being the comet's work. I'd certainly never heard thunder with snow before.

Mam, I hoped, would see sense and say we'd try again tomorrow. Or at least go home and wait for Da.

But no.

Instead, we had to walk behind the cattle from opposite sides of the field. Peg, being smaller, was in charge of the gate.

"As soon as you see us coming straight towards you, Peg, you must open it wide," Mam said. "And don't pull that face. You've to concentrate." Then to me, "Right, Lizzie, let's get shifting."

We started at the top of the field, Mam on the left, me on the right. Wind blew the snow almost horizontally. It had got darker too, and as the grass grew steadily whiter, it was hard to see more than a few feet ahead. Bit by bit we moved down the hill, following the lie of the hedge. There was a knack to it. Keeping yourself quiet and low meant the cattle grew calmer, except I could barely see them anymore.

As I stopped to push the hair from my eyes, I realized I'd gone way off course. Just to my left stood Mam.

"Get back by the hedge," she said, waving me off.

"Can't we stop until the snowstorm passes?"

Above us, flickers of lightning lit the clouds from underneath. It made the whole sky look strange, like milk trembling on a stove. Mam, though, didn't even notice: her gaze was fixed on me. "Remember the deal, Lizzie—the one what we shook on at breakfast?"

I did.

"Good. I'm not scared of a bit of snow, nor should you be. Now move yourself."

So we kept going, first along the shortest side of the field, then slowly up the other, longer side. Soon we had four cattle walking before us.

Then the thunder cracked.

It was louder this time, making the cattle break into a nervous trot. All the while, it grew colder still. My fingers burned red and my chest ached from breathing the icy air. If Mam suffered the same, she didn't show it. Head down, arms out at her sides, she walked like a machine. It was the devil's job to keep pace. Mercy's Midwinter's Eve prediction seemed such silliness now. Mam had more chance of becoming queen of England than she did of dropping down dead.

Yet I still felt a growing unease. Tall trees flanked the top of our field. The rest of it was wide, wide open, and I knew a bit about storms—how trees got lightning-struck, and sometimes cattle too. Now that Mercy's vision had loomed into my head again, I couldn't ignore it.

"Mam!" I yelled. "We won't manage this when it's thundering."

"Stop fussing," she yelled back. "The quicker we round them all up, the quicker we'll go home."

We'd reached the bottom of the field by now. Our four cattle had stopped, legs splayed, eyes bulging, in front of Peg.

"Shall I do the gate?" she cried.

Poor Peg looked so stiff with cold she could hardly lift her arms to heave the bolt.

"No!" Mam shouted back. "Not until we've got all twelve of them."

"But, Mam—"

The lightning cut me short. A bright gold line streaked

through the sky. Seconds later, a great thunderclap followed, so loud I felt the ground shake beneath me.

"We really should stop," I said, hearing fear in my voice.

"Lizzie, I'm scared," Peg whined.

Mam still didn't glance at the sky.

"You're fussing again," she said. "Keep your mind on what you're doing."

Turning on her heel, she marched off across the field. Within seconds she'd disappeared. All I could see now was whiteness. Spinning, sighing, tickling white. Within seconds, my frock and boots were plastered. Flakes got into my eyes and my mouth. How we'd find the other eight cattle in this, I'd no idea.

"We can't go on!" I yelled.

It wasn't about the cattle anymore. Mam was proving herself—to Da and to us. She wouldn't back down, not even when it was dangerous to keep going.

I went after her. Her footprints were all I had to follow; they led me to two steers standing nose to tail in the middle of the field. Behind them, arms wide, was Mam.

My heart sank in despair.

It was madness. Mam even *looked* mad. Her hair, worked loose from its pins, was plastered against her cheeks. She didn't stop to push it back. In one hand she still held her pitchfork. As she inched towards the cattle, they flicked their ears anxiously but didn't move.

"Mam! Leave them be!" I cried.

She took no notice. Her gaze was fixed on those two snow-covered rumps. "Forward!" she cried at the cattle. "Ho! Ho!"

She raised her pitchfork. The cattle bellowed and sprang away across the field.

Then came an almighty flash. Thunder roared directly above us. I cowered in terror. My first thought was for Peg. Turning to rush back to her, I saw Mam. She hadn't moved. Her pitchfork still reached for where the cattle had been. The prongs were blackened, smoke curling off their ends.

"Mam?"

I went to her. Put my hand on her shoulder to shake her. Then came another flash, this time bright blue. There was a crackling sound. The smell of burning. My ears began to sing. A terrible heat poured down my left cheek, my left arm, my leg. My chest seized up. I couldn't breathe. The whole world started lifting and whirling before me. And then a great force threw me clean off my feet.

Chapter 9

WHEN I AWOKE THE BIRDS were singing. I was lying in a bed, the blankets rough and heavy against my skin. A breeze blew in from somewhere, lifting the hair off my forehead. The air wasn't cold anymore: it smelled of spring, though everything else still looked as dark as a winter's day.

The reason for this soon became clear. A damp piece of muslin had been put over my eyes.

"Don't touch!" Peg cried as I went to lift it off. "You've to keep the cloths on. Your eyes are burned."

Her voice made me jump.

"What? I mean . . . where . . . ?" But by now I'd guessed I was at home in my own bed with Peg beside me. I tried to sit up but the pain was too much. The skin on my neck and arms felt like glass about to crack. I lay back, sick and exhausted.

"What's happened to me, Peg?" I asked, when I managed to speak again.

There was an awkward silence.

"You . . . well . . ." She hesitated.

I almost wanted her to lie. Just a little white one, as she often did. But she couldn't do it.

She didn't need to.

In one awful wave, it came back to me—the thunder. The brilliant blue light. Mam with her pitchfork raised and that stench of burning, which, I supposed, had come from me.

"Open the window wider, would you?" I said weakly.

Peg did as I asked. I lay quiet, filling and emptying my chest in long, slow breaths until the pain in my body eased.

At some point I grew aware of sounds from outside—the happy gabbling of my geese, and from Da's workshop, sawing and hammering. Those noises were as familiar as my own heartbeat. They meant life was continuing, that everything was all right. I'd get well again, my eyes would heal, and things would be . . .

"Where's Mam?" I asked.

I heard Peg swallow anxiously.

"Peg?"

"Shh, just rest," she said.

Outside, the sawing stopped. And Da came inside. His footsteps on the stairs were unusually soft. As he came into the room, he brought his always smell of wood chips and sweat. But with the cloth still over my eyes the shadowy shape of him looked smaller, somehow.

"You're awake at last, Lizzie," he said. His voice sounded thick. "The doctor gave you a strong draught."

"Have I been asleep long?" I said, assuming he'd say a day or two.

"Nearly two months. It's April now."

"April?" I spluttered. "How can that be?"

"We thought it best that you"—Da paused—"sleep through the worst of it."

I heard his hesitation: he was choosing his words with care. A tightening sensation grew in my chest. So this *wasn't* the worst of it. Something more dreadful had happened. And I knew what he wasn't telling me, because Peg hadn't either.

"Where's Mam?" I said once more.

For a long while, he said nothing. Peg took my hand, stroking it as if it were a kitten. Da kept clearing his throat, so that in the end I asked again.

"Da? Where is she?"

"The lightning . . . it . . . umm . . . struck your mother first. It went right through her, Lizzie, to hit you."

That fresh air coming through the open window meant nothing now. I couldn't breathe.

"Did she . . . ?"

"She died, Lizzie, yes. The silly, stubborn creature died just to prove a point."

Now he'd started, Da talked on as if he couldn't stop. But his words seemed as if they were meant for someone else. I wasn't sure I was even here, not properly. Inside my head was a big black space that stretched on with no end. It was terrifying.

"I can't bear it," I said. Squeezing my eyes shut, I tried to block everything out. It was impossible. Next to me, Peg had started crying. Da gave a little cough. If he was crying, he did it silently.

"You'll have to bear it, my girl," he said, with a sharpness I didn't expect. "And plenty more besides."

Those next few weeks, it was easier just to sleep. Each hour of each day was a reminder that Mam had gone. In between the sleeps Mercy would visit, pulling up a chair by my bedside and knowing, for once, just to sit and not fill the silence with talk. There were times when I'd listen out for Da. Often I heard hammering and sawing from his workshop, but rarely did I sense his tread upon the stair. It was Peg who brought most of my food, who kept telling me to rest so that my eyes would get better. But the problem with sleeping was the waking part, when, hard as a horse kick, it would hit me all over again.

It was on such a day in May that I woke, in a sour-smelling twist of bedsheets, and knew it couldn't go on like this. It was time to face the world.

By now, the skin on my neck and arms no longer hurt. I dreaded to think what it looked like, though, for it felt tight and unnaturally smooth. Sitting up, I took the cloth from my eyes. I blinked. Rubbed. Squinted. With or without the cloth—it didn't make a jot of difference—I still couldn't see right. My eyes hadn't healed at all.

In panic, I called to Peg.

"What is it?" she cried, clattering into the room.

"What's happened to me? I still can't see!"

"Oh," she said. "I thought that you'd . . ."

". . . get better? So did I."

My sister sat with me as I cried in great, choking sobs. And that made me feel doubly awful, for Peg was just a girl herself. Only now she didn't have a mother—*we* didn't have a mother. I'd opened my stupid mouth at breakfast that day, and when Mam said we'd bring the cattle in, I should've stopped her. Instead I'd gone along with her, and even shaken hands. How foolish we'd been.

The worst part was that I'd survived. And I had to find a way to live with that, starting today.

Eventually, the tears stopped. I wiped my face and snotty nose, and began to get my bearings. There, to my left, was the lightness of the window. Directly ahead was the doorway, lighter too, which I supposed meant it was open. It seemed I could tell light from dark, at least.

"It's no good pretending I'll get better, Peg," I said. "This is it now. This is me."

Slowly, I swung my legs over the side of the bed. All down my left side, the skin creaked and my limbs felt stiff and heavy. I stood up. Everything was gray and swimmy-looking. This wasn't going to be easy. I still needed my sister's help.

"You there?" I asked.

"I'm here," she said, at my side.

"Good." I reached out, and finding her bony shoulder, I gave it a kindly squeeze. "Now, nice and slow, we're going downstairs. I need to get washed, and you're going to help me, all right?"

"Right."

She sounded reluctant, and I guessed why. "You've seen my scars, haven't you?"

"Yes," she said, a bit too brightly. "But they're not *that* bad, really they're not."

I took a deep breath. "Tell me again, properly this time."

Peg groaned. But I got it out of her in the end. One scar ran from just below my jawbone to my elbow. The other went from my hip to the sole of my left foot. They weren't like normal scars at all.

"They're like veins, Lizzie, like the underneath of a leaf," Peg said.

She made them sound almost pretty, which I knew they weren't, though I did appreciate the lie.

*　*　*

We made it down to the kitchen well enough. As Peg went outside to draw water from the pump, I tried to find soap and clean linens. Even in a place so familiar, it was hard. I kept bumping into the table and cracking my shins on the chairs tucked underneath. It made me so angry and teary again I almost called out to Da, whose bangings and thuddings told me he was outside in his workshop.

Then came the sound of footsteps crossing the yard. The doorway darkened. Expecting it to be Da, I stood up shakily.

"I've come downstairs at last," I said, hoping he'd be pleased.

"And you look in need of some help too," a cheery voice replied.

It was Mercy. And oh, was I glad she was here.

Before long, I was washed and dressed, and though still weak, I felt better than I could have imagined.

"Eat," said Mercy, putting a plate of food in front of me. The smell of it—savory, buttery, meaty—made my mouth water.

"It looks proper tasty," said Peg.

Then came a slapping sound.

"Ouch!" Peg squealed.

"Keep your hands off, then! It's one of my mam's best ham hock pies for Lizzie," said Mercy.

For the first time in ages, I smiled—almost. Then guilt swooped down on me like a great black bird. It wasn't just Da and Peg and me who were suffering. Poor Mercy, who'd tended me so kindly, had argued with her sweetheart, Isaac Blake, and then seen awful things in the churchyard. I'd no business to be sitting here smiling. Swallowing a mouthful of pie, I found I couldn't eat any more.

"You knew this would happen to Mam, Mercy," I said, pushing my plate away. "You saw our spirits enter the church that night."

She dropped into the chair next to mine, her arm circling my shoulders.

"Come now, it's just a daft old myth. No one really believes that stuff nowadays."

"Don't they?" I said, thinking how she'd cried. "You seemed to. Or perhaps this awful bad luck is because of the comet."

"Forget all that, Lizzie," Mercy replied. I imagined her batting away centuries of superstitions with a waft of her hand. "See, *fashionable* folk believe in real things that can be proved."

"You've changed your tune."

"Well, why not? Especially now we've got our very own scientist living in the village. Made quite an impression, so he has, though I've not seen him yet myself."

Mercy had spoken of this before, I remembered. The man was moving into Eden Court, and Da had been making shelves for him. It was exciting news by Sweepfield's standards, yet it was also a bit baffling.

"Why would a scientist come from London to Sweepfield?" I asked. "We're miles from anywhere. There's more pigs here than people."

"He's doing secret science work, but no one really knows what." Mercy started shuffling in her seat as if she was smoothing down her skirts. "Anyway, are you well enough to take a walk?"

I gulped, nervous again. "No. Not today."

Mercy, not living up to her name, wasn't about to take no for an answer.

Chapter 10

CROCKERS LANE WAS A ROAD I knew blindfolded. Yet when it came to it, I needed the help of two people to stay on my feet. Mercy kept on my left side, Peg on my right, each holding me firmly by the hand. Halfway down the lane Mercy suggested we walk over the fields instead.

"It'll be quieter, Lizzie. You can take your time," she said.

I think she saw how jumpy I was. All those weeks in bed, I'd felt safe. Hidden. Now I had to face the world, and it terrified me. What if I got lost or fell down or made an idiot of myself? I knew what happened to piglets born blind, or to horses too old to see right. If Mam was here, I'd feel stronger. But she was now just a body in the ground—and I needed to pay my respects.

"I'd like to walk on to the churchyard. It's not far," I said.

Mercy hesitated. "Oh . . . erm . . . very well, if you think you can manage it."

"What's the matter?"

"Nothing," she said quickly. "Nothing at all. Honest."

Last time I'd been on Crockers Lane, it was a bitter cold winter's day. Even today the wind still had an icy bite to it, and the dullness of the light told me there wasn't any sun. But it was spring, according to the calendar. And I tried hard not to think of the budding hedgerows and all the other glorious things I couldn't see. It wasn't easy. Nor was walking past our field where the accident had happened. I knew we'd reached it when Peg suddenly said, "Da sold the cattle to Mr. Henderson, you know."

"Oh." It didn't shock me. But it still hurt to hear it, for it made things more real, more final.

By the time we'd turned left towards the village green, I was beginning to get my bearings. To people who didn't know, we probably looked like any other girls on a morning stroll.

Which, of course, we weren't.

This was Sweepfield. Everyone would know what had happened to Mam and me. We were bound to run into someone who'd say how sorry they were, and I'd feel frightful and want to cry. I began to wonder if I could face this after all.

It was too late to turn back. Up ahead, I heard the clip-clop of horses' hooves and the jangle of a shop bell. There were voices too, people greeting each other in the street. Mercy's hand tensed on my arm.

"Are you ready?" she said.

"I ... I don't know." Suddenly I saw myself as Peg and Mercy saw me: a girl with strange red scars and eyes that didn't work. My frock covered most of the marks, but even a bonnet brim couldn't hide the scars on my jaw and neck. Babies might cry on seeing me. Horses might leap sideways. It made my mouth turn dry.

"Don't worry, that was only Mr. Henderson going into the post office," Mercy said. "Married a year and his wife still works there. My mam says it's all very *modern*."

Which instantly made me think of that stupid blindfold game, and how Mr. Henderson had met his future wife playing it. One person I prayed we wouldn't meet today was Isaac Blake. The thought made me shrivel up with shame.

"There isn't anyone else ahead, not even a dog," Peg informed us.

I sighed in relief. "Good. Onwards, then."

In the main street, Mercy grew more forceful in her guiding. "Watch the pothole to your left," then, "Stop! Horse coming!" and "Step up onto the grass."

Beneath my feet, the road turned to springy turf as we crossed the village green. From here it wasn't far to the churchyard. Church Path lay before us, and beyond that, the place itself. The walk hadn't been too taxing after all. It was good to smell spring grass and hear the birds again. Yet just when I relaxed a bit, Mercy stiffened at my side.

"Uh-oh, bell ringers up ahead," she muttered under her breath.

I braced myself. There'd be condolences now, questions after my health. I'd be polite, of course—they'd only mean well by asking. Then we'd move quickly on.

Except as we got closer, the men fell silent. There were no greetings, no enquiries. In the end it was Mercy who spoke as we went by. "Morning, Mr. Cleave! And to you, Mr. Strawbridge and Mr. Passmore! Isn't it cold today?"

I didn't hear a reply.

"Why are those men staring?" asked Peg, once we were out of earshot.

"Don't know," Mercy said. "They're pointing at us. Look! Keep walking! Don't worry, Lizzie. I'm certain they weren't pointing at you."

Which, I sensed, meant they were.

Once we'd reached the churchyard, I told Peg to run on ahead to Mam's grave.

"Those bell ringers," I said, once she'd gone. "It was me they were staring at, wasn't it?"

Mercy didn't answer.

"I feared it would be like this," I said, tears springing to my eyes. "I should've stayed home."

Mercy patted my arm. "You know what people are like when there's been a tragedy. It'll pass. They'll be gossiping about Eden Court again by teatime."

Sniffing back my tears, I hoped she was right. But it stung to be called a tragedy. I was just about to say so too, when Peg slid to a breathless halt in front of us.

"It isn't fair!" she cried. "I hoped it'd be just us today, but someone else is already at Mam's grave!"

"Who is it?" I asked.

"I don't know. They've got a long, dark cloak on with shiny buttons down the front, and they're proper tall too."

The person didn't sound familiar. Forgetting my own troubles for a moment, I fumbled for Peg's hand. "You'd better show us."

We followed the path that led to the far corner of the churchyard, where the yew trees grew dark and glossy green. The air here was cold, winter air. Beneath our feet damp grass soaked into our skirt hems.

"There, that's the person," said Peg, stopping sharp.

"Oooooh," breathed Mercy.

I'd no idea which direction we were facing. Or how far away from the stranger we were. Or, more importantly, what they'd seen.

71

"Describe them, can't you?" I hissed.

Mercy breathed deep. "Well, it's a man.... No, wait ... it might be a woman.... No, maybe it's—"

"Which is it?" I said, frustrated that I couldn't see for myself. "It can't be that hard to tell."

"It's a man," Peg confirmed. "He's got dark hair combed forward."

I wondered if she'd made that last bit up. Especially when Mercy said, "No he hasn't. He's wearing a curled wig."

"Never mind that now, Mercy," I said. "Tell me what he's doing."

"Umm." I pictured her peering with her eyes all screwed up. "He's writing something down."

"Can you see what?"

"It looks like he's copying from your mam's headstone."

"Are you sure?"

Peg cried, "Hush!"

Then came the crackle of paper, the *swoosh* of a cloak. Footsteps thudded across the grass, away from us to the front of the church and the village green. A blackbird shrieked before the quiet settled heavily around us again.

"Phew! He's gone," said Mercy.

"Back to Eden Court, I expect," I said, because it was dawning on me who this stranger probably was. There weren't many in Sweepfield whose cloaks made that expensive, silken sound.

Mercy gasped. "You think he's the scientist?"

"He might be," Peg agreed. "He looks like a city sort."

Mercy was keen to discuss it some more. But the episode had left me confused. Why on earth would a scientist be visiting my mother's grave? I'd no idea. No idea at all. And right now my mind was too full to take it in.

Holding my hand, Peg led me across the grass to the spot where Mam lay.

"It's a small grave, but it's proper nice. It's got angel's wings on it, see?" said Peg, placing my fingers on the headstone.

Slowly, I traced the curved lines. I tried to think of how pretty they must look, but all I felt was cold, rough stone. The churchyard smelled of rotting leaves, and from the dappled shadows, I supposed we were right under trees. Poor Mam shouldn't have been left somewhere this bleak; she should've been laid to rest in the sun.

Tears rolling down my face, I dropped to my knees. Peg knelt beside me, her elbow and hip pressed comfortingly against mine. We stayed like that until our legs ached and our skirts grew even damper.

"All right?" Peg asked me.

I sniffed. "Just about."

Putting my hand out to push myself up, I felt something lying on the grass. It was a heavy, round, button-sized thing.

"What's this?" I asked, holding it for the others to see.

"That's a brass button." Mercy breathed in sharply. "Or maybe it's a gold one."

"Cor! Let me see!" Peg cried, leaning in close. "It's got a shape on it, like a crest or something. It looks right expensive."

"I bet it belongs to that scientist man. It probably came off his cloak," I said, closing my fist around it.

"He might come back for it," Mercy warned. "Or say he finds out you've got it and comes after *you*?"

The crying had worked loose something knotted up inside

me, and I felt bolder because of it. The worst had already happened: we'd lost our mam. There wasn't much left in the world to be scared of, and that included scientists and bell ringers.

"I want to know why he was visiting Mam's grave," I said, dropping the button into my pocket for safekeeping. "So *we're* going after *him.*"

Chapter 11

THE MAN HAD HEADED IN the direction of the post office, so Mercy said. It was a short walk away across the green. Despite the building's front window being of thick, watery glass, Mrs. Henderson, who stood behind it, saw everything. Even if the stranger hadn't gone inside, she'd be able to tell us who he was.

Mercy was less enthusiastic. "You look tired, Lizzie. Why don't we come back tomorrow?"

I pulled down my bonnet brim to hide my face.

"I'm fine," I assured her.

Yet outside the shop, my newfound courage faltered. The scent of horses was very strong; it was a sure sign the place was busy. Recalling those bell ringers, I had a rush of nerves. Peg let go of my sweaty hand.

"I'll see if he's in there, shall I, Lizzie?"

I didn't know what to do. Perhaps we should come back tomorrow, as Mercy had said. I might feel stronger by then. But then the shop door opened, the bell above it jangling violently.

"Uh-oh," Mercy muttered.

"Is it the man?" I asked, readying myself to speak with him.

The answer was an earsplitting squeal from Peg.

"Oh, Mrs. Pringle!" she cried. "They're so lovely!"

Mrs. Pringle was old and played the church organ rather badly. I'd no idea why Peg was greeting her like a long-lost friend.

"Yes, yes, now if you'd step aside and let me pass," Mrs. Pringle said, as if she was in a hurry to get away.

"But you've got kittens in your basket, Mrs. Pringle! You must let me see."

Which explained everything.

"The ginger one is a dear," Peg chattered on. "Da wouldn't mind if I had one, would he, Lizzie?"

"Umm ... well ... maybe ..." I didn't suppose Da *would* mind. But it was painful to hear the excitement in Peg's voice, when I couldn't see the kittens for myself and share her joy. It was like listening to a conversation behind a closed door.

I tried to take Peg's hand. "Let's go home and ask Da, shall we?" But she tugged me closer to what I supposed was Mrs. Pringle and her basket.

We didn't reach the kittens. The shop bell jingled and another person came out.

I stiffened. "Is it him this time?"

Peg didn't reply. I guessed she was still cooing over the kittens.

"No," Mercy hissed back. "It's ..."

"Mrs. Heathly, good day!" Mrs. Pringle's greeting answered my question.

"You've heard the latest?" Mrs. Heathly said. "'Twas Dipcott Farm's turn last night. All the ducks were took, every last one of them."

I supposed a fox had taken the ducks, which was a shame, though it wasn't *that* unusual round these parts.

"They believe something attacked the horse on its hindquarters. It left a terrible wound. People are saying it's a *bite* mark."

"A bite mark?" cried Mrs. Pringle. "Goodness!"

I listened harder. Mercy did too; I sensed her go very still beside me. We all knew how Sweepfield folks loved to gossip about the weather, about Eden Court, about births, marriages and deaths. But *bite marks*? On a horse's rump? Now, this *was* interesting.

The shop bell rang again. There was a rustle of skirts, a creak of baskets. The *tap tap* of someone coming down the steps towards us.

Mercy jabbed me in the ribs. "*This* is him."

I nodded, drawing breath to speak. Mrs. Heathly got there first.

"Mr. Walton," she said, "'tis a delight to meet you at last. I trust you've settled in up at the big house?"

Mr. Walton? So the stranger had a name, and not a local one either. By "the big house," she clearly meant Eden Court.

"Sounds like he *is* the scientist," I said to Mercy.

I must've spoken louder than I meant to, for Mrs. Heathly then noticed our presence. "Ah, it's the Appleby girls out and about with Miss Matthews."

I tugged nervously at my bonnet brim. "Good day, Mrs. Heathly."

There was an odd little pause. Then, with a curt "Good day," she shouldered past.

"She didn't even look at the kittens," said Peg in disbelief.

"Never mind, dear," Mrs. Pringle muttered. "Now really, you must let me past."

Then she too was gone, and I was left with the distinct sense that we'd just been given the brush-off. Mr. Walton cleared his throat, which made me jump, for I thought he'd gone too.

"So you're the Appleby girls, eh?" he said.

I nodded.

"And you, sir," I said, remembering what I needed to ask, "were at our mam's gravestone just now."

Doof.

A small, hard something hit me on the knee. Doing my best to ignore it, I kept talking. "Did you know my mam, sir? Only if so . . ."

Doof.

I gritted my teeth.

Doof.

I prickled with irritation. Here I was trying my hardest to ask important questions, and someone was throwing stones at us. At *me.*

Mercy cursed under her breath. Without warning, she commenced yelling inches from my ear. "Isaac Blake! 'Tis no good hiding behind the oak tree! I know it's you, you little toe rag!"

"Good gracious, my hearing is ruined!" Mr. Walton exclaimed.

It took me by surprise too—and not just the yelling part.

"You're still not friends with Isaac?" I asked her. I assumed they'd have made up by now.

"Nope. Not a chance." I pictured Mercy, stony-faced, her arms folded. "He tried to make trouble between us, Lizzie, and I'm not having that."

"Perhaps he didn't really mean it. . . ."

Doof.

"Why *is* that boy throwing stones?" Mr. Walton asked.

78

I shrugged, though I'd a sense Isaac was poking fun at me, and it made me hot with anger. "He's the village pest, sir."

"He's a good-for-nothing worm, that's what he is," Mercy added.

I felt a sharp tug on my sleeve. "Isaac's waving at us, Lizzie," said Peg.

"Huh!" Mercy snorted.

I nudged Peg to be quiet, for I hoped Mr. Walton might take pity on us and be good enough to grab Isaac Blake from his hiding place and box his ears. And then we could finally get to the bottom of this gravestone business without any more interruptions.

"Can you tell him to stop?" I said. "And please, sir, why were you in the churchyard?"

"Well, good day to you all," Mr. Walton replied, as if he'd not even heard me. Gravel crunched underfoot as he walked away.

"Sir! Wait! Could you . . . ?" I trailed off.

But he'd gone.

"Fat lot of help *he* was," I muttered.

Doof.

A stone pinged off my forehead. That was it. My temper flared.

"I know it's you, Isaac Blake! What a weedy specimen you are, now that you know I can't get you back!" I cried.

Mercy joined in. "How dare you, Isaac! Don't you ever speak to me again after this!"

"But look—he's beckoning us, or waving, as if he's trying to tell us something," Peg said.

I didn't believe a word of it. Not for a minute.

"It's all right. He's gone," said Peg eventually.

I let out a long breath.

"And good riddance," Mercy muttered.

"But Lizzie, that person . . ." Peg stopped.

"The man? Mr. Walton?"

Silence.

"I can't see if you're nodding, Peg."

"Yes. The man." She sounded very serious. "I think you're definitely right about him being the scientist. That button you found was just like the ones on his cloak."

"I reckon so too," Mercy agreed. "Folks who've seen him say he's awful tall."

"And he *was* mighty tall—tall as . . ." Peg searched for the word. ". . . a giant!"

I gave a nervous smile. "A giant, eh? Did he have huge feet and big hands and a face full of warts?"

"Stop it." Peg started to giggle and Mercy joined in. But I couldn't quite manage it. All I could think of was Mr. Walton stood at Mam's graveside, writing things down. If he *was* the scientist from Eden Court, then what did he want with her?

With *us*?

I'd not the faintest idea.

Chapter 12

OUR TRIP TO THE VILLAGE had proved an unpleasant reminder that life from now on wouldn't be easy. Things were different— *I* was different. And the people of Sweepfield had made me feel it.

"There's bound to be talk," Da said when I told him. "You survived a terrible accident. Folks are intrigued."

"They'd do better to be interested in that Mr. Walton man," I said. "He's a strange one, all right, to be visiting our mam's grave."

Da heaved a long, tired sigh, the sort a person does when they don't quite believe you.

"It's true," I said. "Peg saw him. So did Mercy."

"There's no law against visiting a churchyard, Lizzie. Besides, as I work for Mr. Walton now, maybe he was just showing us his sympathy."

But I didn't much like people's sympathy, especially coming as this did from a stranger: it made me feel pitied. And pity scared me, for it forced me to think of all I'd lost. Grief already gnawed at my edges, and if I let it, it would swallow me whole.

* * *

For the next few days, I stayed home. There didn't seem much point in venturing out just to be stared at or to be a target for Isaac Blake and his stones. Truth was, I felt shaken and very low. So much so, I didn't even get dressed. Hiding away didn't help matters, though: it just made life dreary and dull. So when Mercy stopped by, I tugged on my frock and combed my hair, ready as I'd ever be to face the world—or Mercy, at least.

"Fancy a walk?" I said, tying my shawl before she'd a chance to come inside. "It'll be just the two of us." Da had gone out on carpentry business and taken Peg with him. It was a rare occurrence not to have her tagging along with us.

"All right. Not into Sweepfield, though."

"No, not Sweepfield."

On that we were agreed.

So at our gate we turned right, heading instead towards the main Netherton road. At first, the lane was rough underfoot; I had to concentrate hard. Mercy, her arm through mine, guided me past puddles and ruts made by cartwheels. On reaching the main road, the ground became smoother, and we settled into an easier pace. Though it was another cold, sunless day, the fresh air helped improve my spirits. So did Mercy feeding me barley sugars so sweet they made my teeth ache.

Then, out of nowhere, she said, "It's hens this time."

"Hens?"

"Mrs. Morrison's Speckled Sussexes. All fourteen taken and not a single feather left, so I've heard."

My brain took a moment to catch up. "Weren't some ducks taken from Dipcott Farm the other day? And didn't a horse get bitten too?"

"They did. It was."

I dug my free hand into my pocket. "Then that's an awfully hungry fox if you ask . . ." I stopped. "Oh."

Inside my pocket I found something cold and hard and little. It was, I remembered, Mr. Walton's brass button, the one he'd dropped at Mam's grave. It gave me an idea—one that might make things clearer, and prove to myself that I could still be brave.

"Eden Court's up this way, isn't it?" I said.

"It is—another half a mile or so. That Mr. Walton's moving more belongings in today—bottles of things, ropes and pipes and rolls of wire, so I've heard."

It sounded fascinating. "Fancy a closer look?" I asked.

Mercy stopped. "What, go *into* Eden Court?"

"Not into the house, no." I pulled the button from my pocket and showed her. "Just to the front door to return something, that's all."

"Why, you sly thing!" The admiration in her voice told me she approved.

At the crest of Sweeper's Hill we turned off the main road onto a lane, which I remembered for how the trees arched high above it. From here, Eden Court was only a few hundred yards away, its roofline visible through the treetops.

"Can you see the house? Does it still look like a castle?" I asked.

"It *really* does," said Mercy, a shudder in her voice. "I bet it's got cannons on the roof. Actually, come to mention it, there *is* something up on the roof. I'm sure it wasn't there before."

I felt a twinge of excitement. "What is it?"

"It looks like a flagpole or something, but without the flag."

Which didn't sound that exciting after all.

"Come on," I said, tugging her arm. "Let's see if Mr. Walton is at home."

Minutes later we'd reached the gates. "This is it," Mercy said. "Eden Court."

In my head, I saw the gateposts: gray stone pillars with bird shapes carved into them that Mam once told me were phoenixes. "They're all about hope, those birds," she'd said. "In the story they rise up from the flames, just to prove that even when everything's destroyed, life can begin again."

At the time, I didn't understand what she meant. I wasn't sure of it now either. Life without Mam was full of things I didn't understand: Mr. Walton at her gravestone being one of them.

Then Mercy said, "Oh, I wasn't expecting the gates to be wide-open."

"All the easier for us to get in," I said.

Mercy hesitated. "It doesn't exactly look welcoming, though."

"It never has," I reminded her. "Come on."

We'd only gone a few yards down the drive when from behind us came the thud of hoofbeats. Rapidly, they got louder. I heard the snorts of horses, the slap of reins. Mercy bumped against me. In a tangle of arms and legs, we fell sideways. From the damp, rank smell, I guessed we'd landed in a ditch.

The cart thundered past, so close I felt my bones shake. Then it was gone. All that remained was dust, which settled thickly in my throat.

"He could've blinking well killed us!" I said, scrambling to my feet. "Are you all right, Mercy?"

Nearby, leaves rustled as she stood up. "I'll live."

A quick brush-down and we set off again, more cautiously this time. What I'd forgotten about Eden Court was how short the driveway was. It ended sharply round the next bend. The house, I recalled now, with its stone steps and wide front door, stood not twenty yards up ahead.

"Don't let them see us!" Mercy hissed. "Not yet!"

"Why not?"

Mercy didn't explain. She nudged me into what felt like a bush before squeezing in beside me.

I was a tiny bit annoyed. "What're we doing? Why are we hiding?"

We were so close to the house now, I could hear voices and the jingling of the horses' bits. I tried to stand up, but Mercy pulled me down again.

"That carriage, the one that just nearly killed us, has pulled up outside the house," she said. "They're unloading it now. Stay still a minute so we can see what it's carrying."

"But I came to speak to Mr. Walton."

"Shh! It might be interesting."

I sighed crossly and sat back on my heels. "Go on, then, what can you see?"

"Everything in the back's covered over," Mercy whispered. "No, wait. The covers are coming off. . . ."

"What's underneath?"

"Lots of wooden boxes. They've got lids on, and . . . oh, a servant's just opened one. . . ."

My stomach did a little flip. "What's inside?"

"He's taking things out and holding them up to make sure they're not broken. They look like jars with things in them."

I sat forward. This was getting interesting. It was infuriating too, when all I could see were shadows and light.

"What sort of things?" I demanded. "Pickles? Jam?"

"Don't get sour, Lizzie. I'm doing my best."

"Sorry."

As Mercy went back to explaining, my head filled with images of boxes being unloaded, carried up the front steps and taken inside. The jars, all different shapes and sizes, were of green and blue glass, so Mercy said. There were rolls of wire, stone containers, a crate full of what seemed to be tools.

"Right, that appears to be all of it," said Mercy, getting to her feet. "Let's go and find your Mr. Walton."

From the direction of the house came an almighty crash. There was no mistaking the tinkle of broken glass.

"Oh my! What've they dropped?" I asked, imagining blue and green bottles smashed on the steps.

Beside me, I sensed Mercy stiffen. "That's not a box. That's something else."

She let out a long slow breath.

"Tell me!" I said.

"It can't be. *Can it?*"

This was unbearable.

"You'd better tell me, Mercy Matthews, or I swear I'll—"

She grabbed my arm so hard it silenced me on the spot. "They've dropped a case. Like a glass case with something in it—some sort of stuffed animal. I can't tell quite, but it looks like a giant dog."

"A *dog*?"

"It's probably Mr. Walton's pet."

I had an overwhelming urge to laugh. Or maybe it was nerves. Either way, this discovery about Mr. Walton took me by surprise. So not only was he a mysterious scientist, but he was also sentimental enough to stuff his own pet dog.

"Oh no. What's *he* doing here?" From the way Mercy said it, I guessed someone else had arrived on the scene.

"Who is it, Mercy?"

"Isaac flipping Blake. It's all right, though; they're ordering him to keep back."

"Good. The last thing they'll want is his great feet stomping over all that broken glass."

And if Isaac Blake dared to throw stones at me again, this time I'd give him what for.

"Blimey," Mercy said. "That's an awful lot of pig Isaac's got there."

"What d'you mean?"

"He's handing over a huge pig carcass to one of the servant men."

Now, this *did* make sense, for Isaac's family were pig breeders and butchers. Most of the local meat came from them.

"Perhaps Mr. Walton likes bacon for his breakfast," I said, for I was learning more about this man by the minute.

"But it's still got its snout and trotters on. You'd think he'd have it butchered properly, at least," Mercy replied. "Wait a minute. Why's the man taking it all the way down there?"

"Down where? Oh, tell me, Mercy!"

"He's gone off down a path that seems to run alongside the stables. He's walking *away* from Eden Court."

I shrugged. "Maybe they've got a storehouse down there for the meat."

It was a possibility.

It was also possible, I was beginning to realize, that the meat wasn't meant for Mr. Walton at all.

Chapter 13

ALREADY WE'D LEARNED A THING or two about the mysterious Mr. Walton. Yet we'd still not done what we'd come here to do.

"I'm going to knock on his door and give back his button," I said. "And then, since he didn't answer me the other day, I'll ask him what he was doing in the churchyard." For though the stuffed dead dog showed a softer side to Mr. Walton, I still didn't believe Da's suggestion, that he'd been there to pay us his respects.

Walking the last stretch of driveway, I held tightly onto Mercy's arm. I'd never knocked on such a grand front door before, and it made my stomach flutter with nerves. Yet no one stopped us to ask our business. The place was eerily silent.

"Where's everyone gone?" Mercy said. Then, when we'd nearly reached the steps, she gasped, "Oh!"

A flurry of footsteps rushed towards us. I heard a thud, a crunch as something—or someone—sank onto the gravel.

"Oh my word!" Mercy cried. "It's Peg!"

I stopped in my tracks. *"Peg?"*

It completely threw me.

"What the heck are you doing here? Why aren't you with

Da? And watch out," I added. "There's broken glass all across the driveway."

Peg didn't get the chance to explain herself. More footsteps pounded towards us. Then came a man's voice, terrifyingly angry. "Put that down at once, you little heller!"

Another man joined in. "If you don't drop that this minute, I'll . . ."

There were thuds and grunts and Peg shouting, "Ouch! Get off me!"

It was too much.

"Let go of my sister this minute!" I yelled, rushing towards their voices. But the ground suddenly dipped. My ankle turned sideways and I fell down with a thump.

"Oh Lord, there's another girl!" The man sounded close. "And another one behind her, look!"

They meant Mercy, I guessed, who was now beside me.

"Get up!" she hissed, heaving on my arm.

I staggered to my feet.

"So much for keeping this a secret. It'll be round the village in no time!" said the other man, and to us, "Snooping about, are you, girls? Then you'd best turn round and disappear. Sharpish."

"Not until you let my sister go," I said.

"Gladly," said the man. "Take her home and don't come back."

I expected Peg to rush towards me; she didn't.

"He's let her go," Mercy whispered. "But she's clinging to that stuffed dog creature."

"Peg," I said through gritted teeth. "You've to come immediately."

"It's not right what they've done to this dog," she wailed. "A pet deserves a burial, doesn't it?"

"That's no one's pet!" the man sneered.

Mercy whistled under her breath. "I've never seen a dog that big before!"

As we moved nearer to Peg, broken glass crunched underfoot. In the gray daylight, the men appeared as vague, wide shadows.

"Peg," I said. "Come here, please."

"I don't reckon she's going to let it go," Mercy muttered.

I'd had enough. So too, it seemed, had the men.

"You break that animal, girl, and I'll break you!" one man said.

"Grab it from her," said the other.

Someone gasped. Groaned. I rushed forward, dragging Mercy with me. A boot caught my kneecap. Fists whizzed past my ear. All around me bodies heaved: one of them was Peg's. Grabbing and snatching, I felt hair, shirtsleeves, fingers. And the dry, coarse fur of that enormous dead dog. When, at last, I touched a thin shoulder, I grabbed it with all my might.

"No!" squealed Peg. "Let me alone!"

"Fat chance," I said. "You're coming with me."

I wrapped my arms tight around her wriggling middle. More shouts came. More flying fists. Mercy yanked my sleeve. It caught me off balance. My feet somehow tangled in her skirts and we fell together in a heap—Mercy, me and Peg still squirming in my arms. Where that stuffed dog was now I'd no idea. But she'd clearly let go of it at last.

To our right, a door creaked open. Someone came out. Their boots went *clippety-clip* down the steps, then stopped.

"What THE DEVIL is going on here?" a new voice said.

We scrambled to our feet.

"Crikey," Peg whispered, slipping her hand into mine. "It's the scientist man."

"Bit late to be scared now," I replied. In truth, I was cringing with embarrassment. This really wasn't going to plan.

"Mr. Walton, sir." One of the men addressed him. "We've had a little incident...."

"Quiet, Jeffers!" Mr. Walton snapped. "Clear that glass up. And take the animal inside. I trust the other one is safe?"

"Yes, s-s-sir ... he's already in the stable block, as requested. He came in with the previous cartload."

"Good," Mr. Walton muttered. "We can't afford any more mistakes."

I supposed he meant the glass cases, which would be expensive to replace. Though why anyone would keep a stuffed dog in a stable I didn't know.

The daylight darkened as a shadow loomed over me.

"Ah, Miss Appleby," Mr. Walton said, speaking as if his teeth were clenched. "What, pray, brings you here?" He was struggling to stay polite—and he wasn't the only one pretending. Chin up, shoulders squared, I tried my best to seem brave.

"The other day, sir, we saw you at my mother's grave. Did you know her somehow? Only, I wondered why you were there," I said.

"Your *mother's grave*?" He gave a short, irritable laugh. "You're mistaken."

"No, sir. There aren't many in Sweepfield who look like you."

"I assure you, child, it most certainly wasn't me. Perhaps you should be on your way."

But I wasn't about to be so readily dismissed, not when I knew he was lying.

"After you'd gone I found this button in the grass, and I believe it's yours, sir." My fingers shook as I dug deep into my pocket. In the corners, I found breadcrumbs and bits of hay. The button, however, had vanished.

Instinctively, I glanced down, thinking it must've fallen out when I'd wrestled Peg. All I saw was dark, fuzzy gray: I'd never find a brass button. Nor would Peg or Mercy, who could actually see, not on a gravel driveway. And not with Mr. Walton breathing down our necks.

"So where is this button?" he demanded.

"It appears"—I cleared my throat—"that I've dropped it. I had it, though. I swear."

"She did. I saw it too," Mercy chipped in.

I sensed Mr. Walton's attention fixed on me. "Miss Appleby. I'm at a loss as to why you came here."

"To give back your button, sir. And to ask why you were in the churchyard."

"Yet there is no button, and I've given you my word that I wasn't in the churchyard, so you're clearly wasting your time."

I didn't agree. After all, I'd witnessed his cart being unloaded and a whole pig disappearing down a side path to who knew where. Mr. Walton, it seemed, was a strange man with strange habits. My suspicions about him were growing.

"I have work to do, so if you'd care to leave," he said.

Sensing he'd moved closer, I stepped back.

"And in case you're planning any more *visits*"—his voice became low and threatening—"I'll remind you that what goes on at this house is nobody's business. It's private, secret work.

And you . . ." He seemed to be addressing Peg. "If that animal is damaged in any way, you'll pay for it, understand?"

Pulling Peg to me, I wrapped my arms firmly around her chest.

"My sister meant no harm, sir," I said. "There's no need to frighten her." I was feeling distinctly uneasy myself.

"Do you know what that animal is, Miss Appleby?"

"Why, 'tis a big dog."

He gave another short, bad-tempered laugh. "Indeed, it is a *big dog*. And if it comes to any harm—"

"It's dead," I interrupted. "What harm can come to it?"

Maybe Mercy saw the look on his face, for she started plucking at my sleeve.

"We'll be on our way now. Good day," she said.

It was too late. From the direction of the front door came more footsteps. Then another voice, one I knew very well. I should've realized: if Peg was at Eden Court, it was because Da was here somewhere too.

"Mr. Walton, I've one more question regarding the work-bench. Will you be wanting . . ." Da stopped.

I imagined how it must look to him—the broken glass, the smashed case, Jeffers the servant frantically trying to clear the mess. And us—Peg, me, Mercy—all being dressed down by the man who paid Da's wages. "I didn't mean to run off, Da!" cried Peg. "You told me to wait out in the yard, I know. But then the cart pulled up and I only wanted a quick look."

Though she strained to get free and run to him, I held her fast. She couldn't worm her way out of this one.

* * *

Pa marched us home without a single word. The silence between us bristled like that dead dog's fur. As we went back along the Netherton road, Mercy whispered that people were staring at us. It did nothing to improve my spirits.

Once we were back inside our house with the door firmly shut and Mercy sent home, Da properly lost his temper.

"You pair of idiots! What d'you think you were doing?"

Neither of us answered.

"Well, I s'pect Mr. Walton won't want my services anymore, thanks to you both."

"But, Da," I said. "We only—"

He slammed his fist down on the table. "Quiet! I'm ashamed of you, d'you hear me?"

Peg started to cry. For once, no one comforted her.

It struck me how different Da sounded. How bitter and angry. Everything he said to us these days seemed to be in this same tone.

"Peg, I told you to wait outside while I spoke to Mr. Walton. But, Lizzie, what the heck were *you* doing there?" Da asked.

I kept my gaze down. Whatever I said was going to sound stupid. "Umm . . . I wanted to ask Mr. Walton . . . something."

"This isn't about the graveyard again, is it?"

I shrugged. "Maybe."

"For goodness' sake, the man's entitled to go out in public, isn't he?"

"Well, he gives me the shivers," I muttered.

"Mr. Walton is doing important scientific work. He's trying to find new and exciting uses for electricity. It's truly remarkable what he's on the brink of discovering, so just think of that rather than reasons to dislike a man you barely know."

"Electricity? How?" I couldn't hide my interest. "Like that

other scientist who discovered it could light up a lamp or something?"

"Exactly. Though Mr. Walton says his research will take things much, much further. He's got big plans, you know. One day, when he's a world-famous scientist, we'll all be proud to have him as our neighbor."

I wasn't sure about this last part. Even so, I was intrigued. What exactly *was* Mr. Walton doing at Eden Court? What made his work so top-secret, and so certain to win him world-wide fame?

"The man's a genius, Lizzie—a genius who pays my wages. It doesn't much matter what you *think* of him," Da said. "So just watch yourself, all right?"

Which, as a girl blinded by lightning, was easier said than done.

Chapter 14

THE VERY NEXT NIGHT I woke with a start. The moon shining through the window was so bright it made everything glow a soft, hazy gray. Mam always used to say a full moon made her restless. But that wasn't what had woken me. Outside, a bucket clanked. I propped myself up on my elbows to listen. The geese were making a low keening noise that meant they were nervous. Something was in our backyard.

My first thought was *FOX!*

And it was my fault, I realized in horror, because I'd forgotten to shut the birds up in the barn.

Jumping out of bed, I raced for the stairs. But as my foot missed the first step, I lurched forward, elbows, shoulders, feet bumping the wall on the way down. I landed hard on the flagstones, the wind knocked out of me.

This was a stupid idea.

Yet how frustrating it was to always need another person's help. Like now, as I got to my feet, calling upstairs to Da. Through the ceiling I heard his bed creak as he coughed and rolled over. But he didn't wake.

I tried Peg instead. "Come down! I need you!"

As I pulled on my boots, no one stirred, though something

outside clattered to the ground. The geese shrieked. If I stood any chance of saving my flock, I'd have to handle this myself. Finding the back door, I opened it.

This wasn't a fox—I knew straight away. There was no fetid stink, no half-dead birds still flapping. Not even a squabble or hiss. My heart thumped hard as anything.

The moon made our yard seem almost daylight bright. Maybe it was the comet, still streaking across the heavens, that filled me with a now-familiar dread. Gingerly, I felt my way across the cobbles. Then, to my left, I heard a rustle in the hedge. It sounded absurdly loud, and bigger than any fox. It was, I decided, a person.

I knew I should go inside and shake Da awake. Except there wasn't time. In five big strides, I'd reached the hedge. I kicked it hard. "Come out, whoever you are! And hand over my geese!"

The rustling stopped. Then came a mighty crash, a rushing sound. Someone leapt from the hedge, out into the lane beyond, and was gone.

Who the heck it was, I'd no idea. But they were big, I was sure of it—easily Da's size, and all the heavier, no doubt, for having *my* geese tucked under their arms or slung over their shoulder in a sack.

It was insane to think I should go after them: I'd no idea who I'd be following or what might happen if I did catch them up. Yet the instinct to get my birds back was too strong. Standing here *not* knowing felt even worse. I had to do something.

Once I'd found our gate, I lifted the latch. I tried to ignore the fear that crawled up my limbs. So long as I kept straight ahead, away from the ditches, I'd be all right.

Slowly, purposefully, my feet shuffled forward.

There was no Peg to guide me. No Mercy. No Da. I was alone. I'd almost forgotten what it felt like to do something completely by myself. Amidst the fear was a little thrill of excitement that focused my mind. Whoever had taken my geese, I'd do my best to track them down. The fact that it was the middle of the night might make things harder. But at least there'd be no villagers awake to see me try.

Out in Crockers Lane, I turned left towards the village. Only then did I smell it. Just a waft, then it was gone.

It wasn't sharp like fox. It smelled of wet, musty dog. Of woods and the way fallen leaves smell after rain. Whoever's scent it was had been there in our hedge. It was very unnerving.

The lane itself was shadowy and dark. I walked as fast as I dared, feeling with my feet and concentrating hard. I stumbled often. Finally, as the lane swung left towards the village green, I smelled it again: wet fur, wet leaves, rain. And I felt a fresh surge of fear. This scent, I realized, was more animal than human. I began to wonder if I was following a person at all.

Up ahead lay the village green, its large open space made pale by the moonlight. The strange smell grew fainter. Instead, I caught the salty sweetness of fresh grass. I walked on a few more yards. Now I couldn't smell anything. Or hear anything. The person—or *thing*—had vanished. All I felt was the night pressing in on me.

I told myself to be brave. I'd made it this far. Now wasn't the time to give up. I thought of Mam and how she kept going when times got tough. If I listened hard enough I could still hear her voice inside my head, and it urged me on.

Now I had to decide where to go next. Luckily the church clock had just chimed the quarter hour, so I knew the church was to my right. Which meant the main street with its post office and Mercy's mam's bakery was over to the left. It was in this direction that I decided to head.

I'd gone only a few yards when I caught another waft of that strange, leafy smell. It grew stronger as I walked. Soon I'd passed the post office, which loomed shadowlike in the darkness. And then, as my feet hit cobbles, I knew I'd reached the sharp left turning onto Mill Lane. The smell was at its strongest here. My heart began to pound. At last I was closing in on this *thing* I'd followed. I only prayed my geese were also nearby.

Mill Lane ran very steeply down towards the river. It was lined with flint cottages that clung to the hillside like fungi on a tree. I had to steady myself against them just to keep on my feet. All the while I listened out for the squawk of geese, but instead, to my shock, I heard voices. They were raised and anxious, and coming from lower down the street. As I got closer, I saw pockets of light—the swinging, flickering type that shines from lanterns—and shrank back into the shadows.

"How the devil did it get out?" The speaker was Mr. Walton.

I tried to breathe normally. But the thudding in my chest seemed so loud now, I was sure any moment he'd hear it.

"Sir, we kept the gates shut," said a man. He sounded familiar too, perhaps one of those servants we'd grappled with at Eden Court. "We have to be mighty careful; otherwise it puts the horses at risk."

Horses? Risk?

I recalled then what they'd said yesterday about a second stuffed dog, the one they'd taken to the stable yard. But how could something dead be a threat to the horses?

"And you fed it, as we arranged?" Mr. Walton asked.

Now I was more confused.

"The whole pig, sir," the servant said. "Every last scrap. That village boy's bringing them every day now."

"Then I really don't see how—"

A new voice cut in. "Oh, do be quiet." The speaker was a woman. "This . . . *situation* . . . is about the hunt, not the hunger," she said. "You must understand the nature of what we are dealing with here."

"With due respect, I think—"

"Clearly you don't *think*, Mr. Walton," she said. "Otherwise we wouldn't be here having this conversation now."

There was no comeback. No reply. I didn't even know there was a woman at Eden Court, for this one didn't sound like a housemaid. Whoever she was, she'd put Mr. Walton firmly in his place, and I couldn't help but be impressed.

"Well, I do believe it's passed this way," said Mr. Walton eventually. "Look."

He seemed to be prodding something squelchy and soft.

"Is it dead?" asked the servant.

"Very," said the woman. "There are more carcasses over here. See how their innards have been eaten? A fox would've merely bitten off their heads."

It began to dawn on me what they were referring to. I swallowed queasily.

"Thank heavens it's only a goose. We really must be more careful in future," she said.

Only a goose? If it was one of mine, then that bird had a name, a character. And with growing horror, I wondered what the heck it was that had come into our yard and taken every single bird.

"Fortune favors us for the moment," Mr. Walton replied.

"The villagers are starting to think the Appleby girl is to blame. She has a penchant for other people's animals."

Peg.

In shock, I clapped a hand over my mouth. They were talking about my sister. This was getting stranger and more twisted by the second.

"Appleby? She's the lightning girl, is she not?" the woman asked.

"She is."

They were wrong. Peg wasn't the one hit by lightning; that was me. And Mam.

"Then that's not fortune, you fool!" the woman spat. "That's a considerable *inconvenience*. The last thing we want is *more* attention drawn to her. Or to us."

By now I was so muddled, my head felt ready to burst. Yet, flinching, I remembered Mr. Walton at Mam's grave. How he'd recognized us by our surname that day outside the shop. And how he'd lied about the brass button.

My sense about him had been right. He *was* up to something. And it seemed he had a peculiar interest in us. The question was *why?*

Footsteps came up the hill towards me. The voices sounded suddenly very near. I shrank even further into the shadows and held my breath.

Three, maybe four people passed by so close I smelled the leather of their boots. There was another odor too—sharp and chemical, like the varnish Da used. When they'd gone a safe distance, I breathed again.

Then.

Someone came back towards me. A light was thrust in my face. I recoiled.

"Don't you ever give up?" Mr. Walton hissed in my ear. There was no "Miss Appleby" this time, no cool charm.

"I'm . . . I'm . . ." Lifting my chin, I found the words. "I'm looking for my geese. And there aren't any laws that say I can't."

"Forget your wretched geese. What of our conversation did you hear just now?"

"Nothing," I lied.

"Did you see anything?"

"No! Of course not!" I was amazed he'd even ask.

Further up the street, the woman called to him.

"Oh, do keep up, Mr. Walton! Or are you hoping to deprive me of *all* my sleep tonight?"

He turned to go, then turned back again.

"A word of warning," he said. "If this gets out I'll know it was you, and you'll be sorry."

I smelled something else, then. It was fear, coming off him like fumes.

Chapter 15

BY THE TIME I GOT the chance to tell Da what had happened, it was already too late. Very early the next morning I was awakened by a sound I couldn't place. Groggy with sleep, I rolled over. The noise—feeble and catlike—was coming from Peg's side of the bed.

"Oh no," I groaned, remembering what Mr. Walton had said last night about Peg's fondness for animals. "Tell me that's not a kitten you've got there."

"I had to, Lizzie," said Peg, wide awake and excited-sounding. "Before Da and me went to Eden Court the other day, we were in the village and Mrs. Pringle was at the shop with her kittens again and . . ."

". . . you talked her into letting you have one," I finished. "So you've had it for nearly two days and not told anyone?"

Peg made a "hmmm" sound in her throat.

"And you've hidden it away? How?"

But she didn't really need to answer: Peg had been hiding little animals about the place for years. She was very good at it.

Without warning, a tiny furry bundle was pressed against my cheek.

"Give him a stroke," said Peg. "He's called Spider because he's eaten two already."

I couldn't stay cross. Not when Spider the kitten was as soft as a gosling. No wonder Peg couldn't resist him; after all we'd been through, she deserved a proper pet to love.

"So he's the ginger kitten you liked, is he?" I asked, stroking between his ears.

"No, he's black with white paws. Mrs. Pringle had a few like him, so I didn't think she'd notice that he was missing."

I stopped stroking. "You took him without *asking*?"

"Mrs. Pringle wouldn't let me have one without checking with Da, but he was in the post office at the time. And I *am* going to speak to him. . . ."

"But you haven't yet."

"I will," Peg insisted. "Anyway, I waited for ages for Mrs. Pringle to finish talking about those missing hens. But she went on and on, so in the end I helped myself."

"You stole Spider, you mean."

"No I didn't," said Peg grumpily. "She wanted rid of her kittens. I've done her a favor, really."

"That's not how Mrs. Pringle will see things." It was bound to set tongues wagging too. After what Mr. Walton said yesterday, I didn't suppose this would help.

Before I could say more, there was a knock at our back door. It was barely even light, and I'd an uneasy sense that whoever was out there hadn't come with good news. Da got there first. I scrambled out of bed to hover at the top of the stairs.

"What brings you here in such weather?" I heard Da say, for it was bitter cold still and the rain fell in sheets.

Peg joined me on the landing, resting her head sleepily against my shoulder.

"Who is it?" she said. "What do they want?"

"Shh! I'm listening."

Da's tone of voice changed. "Mr. Henderson, I hardly see what this business has to do with us. Of course we haven't taken anyone's poultry."

Feeling for Peg's hand, I found it and held it tight. This was just as Mr. Walton had said; the villagers suspected Peg of taking their livestock. It was nonsense. Utter nonsense.

"What's happening?" she said, bewildered. "They've not come for Spider, have they?"

I shook my head. "Keep him out of sight, though, just in case."

With Spider safely back in our room, we tiptoed down the stairs, stopping halfway to sit side by side on a step. I dreaded what Mr. Henderson would say next, but I wasn't about to miss it either.

"I'm sorry it's come to this, Jed," said Mr. Henderson, not sounding sorry at all. "But things have reached a head. We have to do something to stop these attacks."

Outside, the noise of falling rain grew louder. Mr. Henderson, still standing on our doorstep, would be soaked through. Yet Da didn't invite him inside.

"What do you propose to do about it?" he asked.

"We'd like to search your barns, if we may," Mr. Henderson said.

Well, he could try, I thought bitterly. He'd not find anything in them, not even our own birds. After last night's encounter with Mr. Walton, I was surer than ever who or what really *was* to blame.

"You see, Jed ..." Mr. Henderson gave a nervous laugh. "I'll get to the point. You know how it's been since ... well ... since your *loss*. People do talk."

Da shifted his feet. I imagined him tucking his hands into his armpits, dropping his chin. He didn't like to fight. But I knew he would if he had to—and that made me more nervous.

"Not all people," Da said. "Just the ones who're keen to judge us for our misfortune."

"Yes, well." Mr. Henderson swiftly moved on. "Our business today regards missing livestock—hens, ducks . . ."

"And geese." I stood up, unable to stay quiet any longer. "Ours got taken last night, Mr. Henderson, so it's no good coming here thinking Peg's to blame when she was upstairs fast asleep at the time."

"Why, I never mentioned your sister by name!" he said, sounding flustered.

He didn't need to. The fact he was here at all was enough.

"You've seen that hole in our hedge, have you?" I said, thinking of what had hidden there last night. "Something escaped through it with our geese."

"It's hardly proof. A badger could've made it."

"A badger? Mr. Henderson, what was out there was huge!" I cried.

He didn't reply. Instead, he addressed Da again. "So if we could check your barns, Jed, it would clear up any misunderstanding."

The doorway grew lighter as Da turned round. "Did you know about this, Lizzie? Why didn't you tell me?"

Peg's hand in mine felt hot and sticky. Her breath was coming fast.

"I'd heard something about what folks have been saying," I muttered. "But how can it be Peg who's taking animals when our birds got taken as well?"

Da didn't answer.

106

Here in the light of day, I knew I should tell him all of what had happened last night. And I very nearly did. But if I shared Mr. Walton's secret, he'd come after me; I was sure of it. So the words stayed jammed in my throat.

Peg began to sob. "Whatever the man says, it wasn't me!"

"Hush, my sweet," said Da, coming over to us and scooping Peg into his arms. "We know it wasn't you. It's all a big mistake."

From the doorway, Mr. Henderson coughed. There were shufflings from outside: other voices, other restless coughs. With a sinking feeling, I realized Mr. Henderson wasn't alone.

"My men and I are ready, Mr. Appleby," he said, confirming my fears. "Shall we start with the barn nearest the gate?"

There was no more "Jed": it was surnames only. Da must've noticed it too. He stayed close to me and Peg.

"No one is to search my barns," he said. "My daughter has done nothing wrong. You're mistaken in coming here."

Mr. Henderson huffed irritably. "Very well. I can't force a search today. But if necessary, we will return with a warrant."

The men left soon after that. Then Da did too, heading off to work on the commission for Eden Court, which he'd talked his way into keeping, despite us. Poor Peg was still upset. Dragging me to the nearest chair, and though she was too big to do so, she climbed onto my lap and burst into a fresh bout of tears.

"I didn't do it," she sobbed. "I didn't take any poultry. Everybody blames me and it isn't fair!"

"Hush, I know you didn't."

"The whole village must hate me. I'm not lying, Lizzie, honest I'm not."

"I know, I know," I murmured into her hair.

By the time she'd grown calmer, I felt the opposite. My

brain was all awhirl. A large animal had escaped from Eden Court and was attacking poultry, of that I was pretty certain. I needed not to be scared but to tell someone what I knew. Trouble was, I'd no idea who.

Not Da, who'd made it clear what he thought of loose talk concerning Mr. Walton. And though Mercy might listen, she'd never hold her tongue. Times like these, I missed Mam so much it hurt. She'd listen. She'd believe me. She'd also know just what to do, and be bold enough to do it.

All the crying had left Peg exhausted. Through the fabric of her shift, her skin felt hot and humid. I hoped it wasn't a fever coming on.

"Go back to bed and cuddle up with Spider," I said to her, easing her off my lap. "I'll wake you in a while."

I listened to her heavy footsteps climb the stairs. Then to the creak of floorboards, the shuffling covers, her murmuring voice as she spoke to her kitten. When a hush finally settled, I got to my feet. There was laundry to wash, floors to sweep, the stove to tend. But I couldn't settle to any of it. Instead, I went outside.

Head bent against the rain, I walked towards our hedge. Just to check. Just to be doubly certain last night wasn't a bad dream.

Sure enough, on the ground nearby were leaves and broken twigs that fidgeted beneath my feet. By the gate was a hole. It was way bigger than any badger would make. Against my fingers, I felt the rough ends of newly snapped hawthorn where whatever it was had smashed its way out into the lane. That strange damp smell lingered too.

What had been here last night was definitely not my sister. Nor was it even a person. It was, I recalled with a shudder, something that ate goose innards raw, which Mr. Walton wanted kept secret from the world.

Midmorning, I took Peg up a cup of tea. Much of it sloshed down the front of my frock as I bumped my way upstairs, but I dearly hoped she'd drink what was left. The last thing we needed was for her to be ill.

Outside, the rain had turned to sleet. I found our bedroom window easy enough—icy raindrops beat against it like grit. Putting Peg's tea on the sill, I sidestepped to the bed.

"Wakey-wakey, Peg," I said. She didn't reply.

"I've brought you some tea, sleepy."

She still didn't speak. Nor did she move, or groan, or snore. I felt my way up the bed. First her side, nearest the window. Then mine. Spider was there, all curled up in a ball. But no Peg. The covers were cold to the touch.

My stomach twisted uncomfortably. Perhaps she'd fallen out of bed. Perhaps she lay fainted on the floor. Dropping to my knees, I reached under the bed, finding only handfuls of dust. I checked the rest of the floor, behind the door, the chair.

Nothing.

"Don't hide from me," I said. "'Cause it isn't funny."

I started to feel very uneasy. It wasn't like Peg to take herself off. And surely I'd have heard her if she had? Stumbling downstairs again, I went out into the yard. The sleet fell sideways in the wind.

"Peg?" I called, pushing hair from my face. "Where've you gone to?"

The cobbles were slippery underfoot. I stepped in puddles, slid in mud, but found my way across to the main barn and heaved the door open wide.

"Peg! Enough of this, now! Come out, please!"

Over to my right, something rustled in the straw. I held my breath. It moved again. Very fast. Very light—like a rat, not a nine-year-old girl.

I pulled the barn door shut and leant against it. I didn't know where to look next. But I realized the gut-churning truth: Peg wasn't here. She wasn't hiding either.

Chapter 16

"WHAT D'YOU MEAN, SHE'S GONE?" said Da, when I went to his workshop to tell him.

There was a thud and a rattle as he put down his tools. He clicked his tongue too, which meant he wasn't best pleased. Generally when he was working, Peg was my responsibility. I'd failed in that *and* I'd disturbed him in his workshop, and it made me feel pretty useless.

"She won't have got far," said Da. "She'll be in the house somewhere, won't she?"

I detected the coolness in his tone, the disappointment that I'd not quite measured up. It'd been there since Mam had died, and I'd just made it worse.

"Tell me what happened," he said.

"She ... she ... was upset and went to bed and now she, well, she isn't there."

"Maybe she's gone off to do laundry. Perhaps she's up in the orchard hanging it out to dry."

But we both knew Peg didn't do laundry. Last time she'd tried, her frock shrank to doll-sized and she'd sworn never to touch a bucket of lye again.

"It's sleeting," I said. "Not even Peg would put out washing in this weather."

Da sniffed. Then came the sound of him putting on his jacket. "Still, we'd better have a look, hadn't we?"

So we tried the orchard first. But it was so windblown and cold, it was obvious she wouldn't linger there. Back inside, we called and called Peg's name to no avail. The house was empty. All the while, my discomfort grew.

"She'll have gone to the village, I s'pect," said Da, though he was sounding increasingly concerned.

Then up in our bedchamber, I made another discovery. Peg's woolen shawl, usually flung across the chair, wasn't there. Nor were her stockings or her nightgown. The sixpence she kept under her pillow had gone too. The only thing she'd left was Spider, who'd woken up and was following me around, mewling for food. Though I tried my best to keep him out of Da's way, it wasn't long before the kitten was discovered. Da didn't take this news well either.

"What's got into you both?" he cried. "Why didn't you tell me?"

"I only found out myself this morning." I also wanted to point out that Peg had been out with *him* when she'd taken the kitten, not me. But it didn't seem the right time to say so.

"Well, it doesn't look good for Peg, not now people are talking about all this poultry going missing. And if she has run off, that just makes her seem guilty, doesn't it?"

"She was upset about being blamed," I said. "She thinks everyone in Sweepfield hates her. Honestly, she sobbed her poor heart out."

I felt truly terrible. What sort of big sister was I to let Peg get wrapped up in all this? I had to find her, and tell her everything would be all right and that we'd clear her name.

"It's Mr. Walton who's behind all this," I blurted out. "There's some animal he's got that escaped and ate our geese. It's done it before too, but he's letting Peg take the blame."

Da cussed under his breath. For a split second, I thought it meant he believed me. And I was about to tell him more too, when he said, "That's enough, Lizzie."

Tears of frustration sprang into my eyes. "Won't you even listen?"

"No, because we need to find Peg, all right?"

"It is true, though, Da. I'm not making it up."

"I've not got time for this now, Lizzie," he snapped. "I'm going to ask in the village. Someone must've seen her or taken her in."

I wiped my tears on my sleeve. I'd tell him all about what a *genius* Mr. Walton was, even if I did have to wait for the right moment.

"What shall I do?" I asked.

"You stay here in case she comes back," Da said. "And for once do as you're told."

It was late evening when Da returned. Straight away I knew Peg wasn't with him. There was only one set of footsteps, and when he dropped into his seat by the fire, he gave an exasperated sigh that said more than any words.

"No one's seen her," he said eventually. "It doesn't make sense. People don't just vanish."

I thought of all those ducks and hens, and how our geese

had gone too. Da was right; things didn't just vanish. They got taken. Often by people or creatures who thought it was their right to do the taking.

This, though, was different.

Peg had been upset, enough to grab her clothes and leave. Not simply down the road, but somewhere where we couldn't find her—all because of these awful rumors. I kept imagining her broken-limbed in a ditch or falling under the wheels of a stagecoach. It wasn't much help. We had to think of where she might be heading.

Da didn't sit still for long. Getting up again, he threw open the back door. I joined him in the doorway. The rain had passed, leaving the night clear and cool. Our yard was all gray stone and dark shapes.

"The comet's still up there, is it?" I asked.

Da nodded. "'Tis bigger, if anything. Got a grand tail on it too."

Which was how it'd looked on Midwinter's Eve, a mighty tadpole shape burning through the heavens. It had been spectacular. And that same sense of dread I'd felt then still hung over me.

"Why's all this happening to us, Da?" I asked. "All these bad things? Is it, like folks say, because of the comet?"

He took a deep breath through his nose. "People round here are superstitious, Lizzie. First it was about the comet, then all this strange weather. And that day you got struck? It was a freak storm. Lightning in a snowstorm in January *is* mighty rare, so in a way it wasn't a surprise that it got people talking and wondering why it happened to us."

We'd not spoken of that day before. And now we were, I felt as if I'd been dragged from a cave, blinking at the daylight.

"And," he said, "I'm not sure how to put this, but the talk's not just been about Peg. It's been about you too."

My stomach dropped away.

"What d'you mean?" Yet I knew exactly. I'd sensed those bell ringers gawping. I guessed why Mrs. Heathly had been unfriendly, and perhaps even why Mrs. Pringle didn't really want Peg to have a kitten. I knew that Mercy, out of kindness, had tried to keep me away from the village, though it didn't prepare me for hearing Da say it.

"Your mother died, but somehow you survived," Da said. "Here you are, scarred and blind, and when people see you it reminds them of what happened. It *unsettles* them."

"Do you feel like that too, then?" I asked. "Is that why you've been distant with me?"

He sighed, deep and weary, in a way that made him sound old.

"No, Lizzie, I don't and it isn't," he said. "You went along with your mother that day when it clearly wasn't safe. She had many strengths, your mam, but she was stubborn as a donkey. I just hoped you'd have more sense."

The disappointment was there in his voice. Again.

I didn't think I'd sleep a wink that night. Nor did I bother going to bed. But the next I knew, I'd woken stiff and sore in a chair by the fire with Peg's kitten curled in my lap. It was dawn. Someone was hammering on our door. This time it wasn't Mr. Henderson. Mercy was on our back step, having run all the way from the village, and was now almost too breathless to speak.

"I've news," she gasped. "Peg was seen . . . late last night . . . getting on . . . mail coach . . . Bristol."

My legs went weak with relief.

"Oh thank goodness!" Though I didn't understand. "But *Bristol*? Why would she be going there?"

Or, come to think of it, why *wouldn't* she, especially after how the people of Sweepfield had behaved towards her?

Bristol.

In my mind's eye it was a place of tall brick houses and wide pavements where well-dressed, feather-hatted ladies walked. The whole city would be abuzz with talk of new ideas. They wouldn't blame an innocent little girl if their hens went missing. Perhaps they didn't even *have* hens.

Then the gate clicked again. The footsteps, slow and heavy, were Da's. He'd been out all night scouring the fields for Peg.

"Da!" I cried. "We've news!"

He rushed over. "Where is she? Is she all right?"

Mercy repeated what she'd told me. Then Da asked her to tell it again, holding my hand and trembling from head to foot as she did so.

"Bristol?" he kept saying. "Why would she want to go to Bristol?"

But it was dawning on him too. Bristol was only twenty-five miles away, and coaches that went there and on to London traveled the Netherton road every day. It'd be easy enough to get to. And perhaps in such a busy place, Peg wouldn't stand out and be talked about, but could melt into the crowds. I had to admit it sounded appealing.

"Who saw her?" I asked.

"The man from the flour mill," Mercy said. "He came just this morning with our delivery. Said he saw her getting on the Bristol coach."

"He's certain it was her?" asked Da.

"He said she had this puff of blond curls and was wearing a green frock with a dirty apron over it. And that she gave the horses a pat before getting on board."

It had to be Peg. Especially the last part.

"How would she pay the fare?" Da said.

"She had a sixpence under her pillow," I told him. "She found it in the gutter and kept it, though she claimed she'd earned it in the summer clearing hay."

It was another little Peg lie.

"Was she with anyone else?" I asked Mercy. "Did she seem upset?"

"I'm sorry, I don't know any more. I'd better get back before Mam thinks I've run off too. She needs me in the shop today. She sends you both this and her prayers." Mercy handed me a still-warm pie. Then she was gone.

Moments later Da was leaving too—to Bristol, he said, to find Peg and bring her home. Though not before he'd scratched out a note and pressed it into my hand.

"Take this to Eden Court, Lizzie. It explains where I've gone and why it might delay my work a day or two."

"Eden Court?"

"Yes. Give the note to Mr. Walton."

I gulped. "Mr. W-Walton? Won't the footman do?"

"No, poor Mr. Jeffers is run off his feet up there. He'll stuff that piece of paper in his pocket and forget it until suppertime. It must go directly to Mr. Walton."

"Oh." I turned the note over in my fingers. "Right."

"And be polite, won't you? I'm lucky Mr. Walton wants to employ me after what happened last time you went there."

My cheeks grew hot at the memory.

"Take the main road, and mind you keep close to the

hedge. Come straight home; no going to Mercy's when she's working. Do it this morning, if you will."

I nodded, trying to look attentive. I was desperate to prove to Da that I *could* do something properly. But the idea of going to Eden Court alone made me feel very nervous, especially if I had to see Mr. Walton, who'd distinctly told me not to "visit" again.

"Da," I said. "I'll be all right, won't I?"

"You'll be fine, my girl," he said. "You might be as stubborn as your mother, but you're brave like her too."

Though he didn't kiss me, his words, at least, were something. The gate clicked shut behind him. Then he was gone.

It was too early to go to Eden Court. Fashionable households didn't rise before ten, Mercy once told me. So I picked up some sewing, then put it down again. I added wood to the stove, brought in armfuls more from the barn, played with Spider and a piece of string. Nothing seemed to settle me. In the end, I grabbed my shawl and stuffed Da's note in my pocket.

Never mind what time fashionable people rose. I was up and awake. Unlike before with the brass button, this time I'd make sure Mr. Walton's delivery reached him.

Chapter 17

JUST WHEN I WAS HOPING to find the gates to Eden Court open, they were shut. A good shake didn't shift them. The bolt was pulled across with a chain wrapped twice around it. What Mercy said about this place was true: it really wasn't welcoming.

Racking my brains for another way in, I walked a little to the right of the gate. There were no hedges to squeeze through, no fences to climb, just a flint wall that seemed to run on forever.

I tried hollering instead. "Anyone there? I've got a message for Mr. Walton."

The trees groaned and whispered in the wind. It was cold too—a shivery cold that sank into your bones. I hugged myself, but it did little to warm me. The sooner I delivered this note and went home again, the better.

In the end, I waited an hour or more just for someone to appear. I wasn't expecting that person to be Isaac Blake. I recognized his voice straight away: "Same time tomorrow, Jeffers?"

"Aye, same time, same amount of pig," said this Jeffers person. I knew his voice too: he'd been here last time unloading the cart with Mr. Walton the night my geese were taken, and was the footman Da had mentioned.

Though I was still sore with Isaac for the stone-throwing business, at this moment I needed his help. Or at the very least for him not to pick on me again. So once I heard the gates rattle open, I went over. I was too late. There was a clunk as the bolt slid shut again, then fading footsteps as Jeffers disappeared down the drive.

"Well, well," said Isaac, spotting me. "If it ain't Lizzie Appleby. What you doing round these parts?"

I bristled slightly at the friendliness of his tone. "You'd better not start chucking things at me today."

"I didn't mean it badly," he said. "Honest, I didn't."

"Joking again, were you?" I said, thinking back to the blindfold game.

"No, I was warning you, or trying to. You want to be careful who you're talking to, Lizzie. That Mr. Walton ain't what he seems."

"Hmmm." Peg had said as much, hadn't she? But even if Isaac *was* warning us, I still didn't understand why he'd had to throw stones. I did know what he meant about Mr. Walton, however.

"Well, anyway, I need to deliver a note for Mr. Walton," I said, checking for the square of paper in my pocket.

"Jeffers'll take it for you. Hullo! Jeffers!" As he called to the footman, I covered my ears so as not to be deafened.

"If he could just let me in the gate . . ."

"Ho! Jeffers! Ho! Where's the chap got to?"

"Da says Jeffers is mighty busy."

"He is—like a madman." Then Isaac dropped his voice.

"Since they've taken over the house there's been some funny goings-on. They've put this pole on the rooftop. It sticks up so tall it'll get lightning-struck if they're not careful."

"Oh, really?" I said, trying to sound normal, when the mention of lightning made my guts churn. "Mercy said it looked like a flagpole without the flag."

"She's right, it does." He gave a little sigh. "I wish she'd talk to me again, Lizzie. I really do care for her still, you know."

I hadn't come here to listen to Isaac's lovesick mooning. "Well, that's between you two, not me," I said briskly. "What are you doing here, anyway? I thought Mr. Walton wasn't to be trusted."

"Ah, but this is different. It's business."

"More pig carcasses?"

"How d'you know about that?"

"We saw you delivering one the other day—well, Mercy did. So Mr. Walton's been ordering a lot of bacon, has he?"

"Not bacon, Lizzie—he wants the meat raw. I've brought another whole pig's carcass today. Can you believe it—he wants the same every day."

I was very certain that the meat wasn't for Mr. Walton. It was being fed to that thing that killed my geese, that hid in our hedge and then ran all the way to the village and down Mill Lane smelling like wet leaves. I felt sure of it. So sure it made the hairs on my neck tingle.

"Mind you, Mr. Walton's got guests staying, which might explain why he wants so much meat." Isaac paused. "But I've been thinking about that missing poultry. And that poor horse what got bitten on the rump. I don't know if it's all connected. . . . You've gone awful pale, Lizzie. You all right?"

I didn't get a chance to answer. The thud of footsteps told me Jeffers had reappeared at the gate. "You forgotten something, Master Blake?"

"Lizzie here's got a message for Mr. Walton." Isaac nudged me. I stumbled forward but kept my hand in my pocket.

"I promised I'd take it to Mr. Walton directly," I said.

Jeffers gave a superior sort of laugh. "I don't think so, missy. He's entertaining guests from London. He won't want to be bothered by the likes of you."

It was tempting just to give Jeffers the note. Then I could avoid Mr. Walton altogether and go straight home and shut the door. But what if Da was right and the footman forgot to hand it over? He'd insisted I deliver it myself, and I'd said I would.

"It's urgent. It's about the workbench my da's making for him. It's very important that I take it straight to Mr. Walton without delay."

Jeffers seemed to consider it. "I can't deliver it right this instant. I'm busy doing—"

"Exactly," I said, seizing my chance. "So let me in and I'll do it."

Jeffers continued contemplating.

"Please, Mr. Jeffers," I said, when I couldn't bear it anymore. "I'll be proper quick."

"I'll go with her," said Isaac. "Just to make sure she don't lose her way."

I glared in his direction. "I'll be fine."

Jeffers, though, thought this was a good idea. And I confess a little part of me did too.

"Five minutes, then you're out," he said.

The chains came off and the gates groaned open. When

they clanked shut behind us, it made me flinch. I didn't dare think what was shut in here with us.

Jeffers took us to the front of the house. He began deliberating again, this time about which door we should call at.

"It's not right for you to knock at the front door, but the kitchens are—"

A shout from behind cut him short: "Oi! Jeffers! You coming to help me clean these boots or taking the day off?"

"Five minutes, that's all," Jeffers said, and left us.

I breathed deeply to steady myself.

"Right," I said to Isaac. "Let's get this done."

Taking my arm, he guided me to the front door. He wasn't as gentle as Mercy, and he went a bit fast up the steps. But he placed my hand on the door knocker rather than taking over and doing it himself, which was the sort of help I liked.

I rapped three times. Then we waited for what felt like an eternity. In a house this vast, it might be ten minutes of brisk walking along passageways and down stairs to reach the door. Or perhaps they simply hadn't heard.

Just as I went to lift the knocker again, rapid footsteps approached from the other side of the door. I expected it to fly open. Instead came the sound of bolts being drawn back: I counted five at least. Then a key clicked in its lock, turned, clicked again. At last, the door opened just a crack—I could tell by the little creaking noise it made.

"Yes? What're you wanting?" said a woman's voice, a maid, I supposed. It wasn't the person who'd been with Mr. Walton on Mill Lane.

I straightened my shoulders. "I've got a message for Mr. Walton. It's from my da, who's making a workbench for him."

"I'll see he gets it," the maid said.

There was a pause. Isaac nudged me, so I guessed the maid was waiting for me to hand it over.

"I'm to deliver it myself," I said.

The door creaked again as she opened it a little wider.

"Are you, now? Fancy that." I imagined her eyeing me up and down.

"Lizzie, just give it to her. Jeffers'll be back any minute," Isaac said.

I didn't budge.

"Could you take me to Mr. Walton, please?" I asked.

"I ain't got time to take you anywhere," she said, "not with a house full of flipping guests."

Isaac must've done something clownish, for she suddenly laughed. "All right. Very funny. You'll find Mr. Walton down by the stables—he likes to make sure the animals are fed proper."

"Animals?" Instantly my brain filled with creatures capable of killing ducks and hens.

"I meant *horses*," the maid said, as though I was stupid.

She shut the door with a slam.

"Why'd you have to say that?" Isaac hissed as we headed towards the stables. "You've made us look suspicious."

"Think about it," I hissed back. "All that raw meat you're bringing here, all those missing birds. She said *animals*, not horses. *That's* suspicious."

"True, it might be."

"You said yourself something queer's going on here, and I'll tell you this, Isaac, my sister's been catching the blame."

I told him then about Peg running away to Bristol.

"She's heartbroken," I said, a lump in my throat. "She swears she didn't take anything apart from a kitten. My da's

124

gone off looking for her, which is why he can't work for Mr. Walton today and I'm here delivering this pesky note."

"Poor Peg. That ain't right," Isaac muttered. "That ain't right at all."

He sounded as if he meant it too.

As we walked on, the gravel became beaten earth beneath our feet. Leaves brushed against me. The light flickered and grew darker. We were, I guessed, on a narrow path that wound between trees. Perhaps it was the same path Mercy mentioned the other day—where that man carrying a pig carcass had gone, and I'd thought might lead to a storehouse.

"Where are these stables, then?" I asked Isaac as we walked on.

"They're down here somewhere. Keep going."

But I was beginning to get a bad feeling about this. "I thought you knew where they were."

"I ain't been down this path before. I deliver my pigs directly to Jeffers."

"So we're lost, then?"

"Not lost, just . . ."

A noise up ahead stopped us dead.

"What was *that*?" I whispered.

It sounded like a person crying. A child.

The noise came again. It seemed more animal now, perhaps an owl or a fox. Only it wasn't that either. Then it came again, long and low, and it made me think of pain or fear or deep, dark despair.

"We ought to go," said Isaac.

"Shh! Listen." But though the sound had stopped, there was no mistaking the smell that wafted our way. It made my heart beat fast.

"I'm going to find out what's making that noise," I said.

"Wait, Lizzie," Isaac said, holding on to my arm. "Don't do anything stupid."

The cry came again. This time it made me think of dogs howling. Perhaps it *was* a dog. There'd been a dead dog up here in a glass case, hadn't there? And there was another one Mr. Walton kept near the stables. Yet dogs didn't smell like the woods.

As we listened, the animal howled on and on.

"It sounds dangerous, Lizzie," Isaac warned.

"Sounds sad to me."

"Well, we should keep back just in case."

I rolled my eyes. For all his swagger, Isaac was turning out to be a bit of a fusspot.

"I don't see what it's got to do with us anyway. The animal down there is in a pen," he said. "It's not roaming Sweepfield, helping itself to other people's livestock."

I clenched my fists. Either Isaac was a complete half-wit or he really didn't know.

"And that creature you speak of," I said, "has been escaping."

Chapter 18

THERE WASN'T TIME TO EXPLAIN. Someone was thundering down the path towards us. Isaac gave me a shove.

"Quick! Get in there!"

Before I could object, I staggered sideways. Straw rustled against my feet. The sweet smell, the sudden darkness told me I was in some sort of barn.

"What are we doing?" I said. "What about finding Mr. Walton?"

"Wait there a minute and keep quiet," Isaac whispered.

"But what . . . ?"

A shadow flitted through the lighted doorway: Isaac had gone. And he'd left me here alone, which certainly *wasn't* the type of help I needed. Arms folded, toe tapping, I waited. Waited some more.

I supposed he was outside somewhere, talking his way out of trouble. Yet time passed and Isaac didn't come back. As I listened out for him, all I heard was a *thump-thump-thump*ing coming from nearby. I didn't pay much attention at first: I was busy wondering when to give up waiting and try finding Mr. Walton by myself.

The thumping continued. It was coming from underneath

me, I realized. I wasn't just hearing it now but *feeling* it through the soles of my feet. I supposed it was rats or someone moving boxes in a cellar. Stepping aside, I tried to ignore it. But it kept on.

Thump-thump-thump.

Intrigued, I cleared the straw with my foot. The noise grew louder. I thought I heard a voice calling faintly too, and knelt down to listen. The floor was brick, and set in it, just where I'd been stood, was a square hatch about half the size of a door. The thumping sound had come from here.

It wasn't loud or strong. It was, I realized, the sort of noise a small fist would make.

"Who's there?" I said, leaning in close to the hatch.

A small whimper came in reply.

I knew that sound. That voice.

But it couldn't be.

Sitting back on my heels, I shook my head to clear it. This didn't make sense. Peg had gone to Bristol. She'd been seen getting on a coach. Da had gone after her. "Peg?"

There was another *thump-thump-thump.*

My heart began to race. I crouched again over the door, pressing my ear to it. "Peg? Are you there? Answer me!"

I heard a snuffling, snotty sound, like a person with a cold. With growing certainty, I felt sure it *was* my sister.

I tried to stay calm. "Peg? Now listen to me. I'm going to get you out of there, all right?"

I searched the trapdoor for a handle; there wasn't one, but there was a catch. With a click and a snap, it sprang back. Yet there was nothing to pull on to open the door. All I could do was slide my fingers underneath the edges and try to pry it open. But the gap was too small. The wood pinched my fingertips. Splinters dug under my nails. There had to be another way.

"Peg? The door might open from your side. So I want you to push upwards, as hard as you can," I said. "On the count of three. One . . . two . . . three—"

Even then, I wasn't ready. With a great *whoosh,* the door flipped open. Dust flew into my face, and with it a waft of dank air. And then some grabbing, scratching, squealing thing snatched my skirt hem and pulled so hard I toppled forward. For a split second, I wondered if it *was* Peg after all.

A frightened voice cried, "Lizzie!" and I knew then it was her. But we were locked into a ridiculous knot of skirts and arms, and I couldn't get free. Peg wouldn't stop wriggling either.

"Let go of me so I can get hold of you properly," I cried.

"Oh, Lizzie, it really is you! You've come for me!"

"I have. But I need you to be still for a moment."

Peg did as I asked. But the suddenness of it made me lose my balance. There was nothing underneath me now. Arms flailing, I fell down. And down.

I landed on something soft and springy. Above me, the hatch slammed shut, and a pair of sticky arms flung themselves around my neck.

"I've been shut down here and it's awful! Please, take me home."

"Let me breathe!" I gasped as Peg sobbed into my hair.

Somehow, I got us both into a sitting position. My insides still felt as if they were floating, but I wasn't injured. I'd landed on what seemed to be a bed.

"Are you all right?" I asked.

Feeling Peg's head nod against my neck, I sighed in relief. "Good girl." I hugged her. "Let's get out of here, shall we?"

The only light was a faint glow that seemed to come from a rush lamp. The room felt chill and smelled strongly of damp. Easing Peg off me, I stood unsteadily on the bed. The ceiling was low; I felt along it until I found the hatch again. If Peg had pushed it open by herself, then it'd be even easier with two of us.

"Stand next to me," I instructed Peg. "Now, one, two, three . . . push!"

The hatch wouldn't budge. We tried again, heaving and huffing till my arm muscles burned. But it stuck fast. Then I remembered the catch—that stupid, click-and-snap catch. Once the trapdoor slammed shut, the catch would've closed. And the only way of opening it would be on the other side.

The first waves of panic hit me.

We were locked in.

"Hullo? Isaac? Can you hear me?" I yelled, praying he'd finally come back and was up there wondering where I'd gone.

If anything, the silence grew thicker and I sensed we were deep underground. I really didn't like being trapped down here.

"As soon as Isaac comes back, he'll let us out, I promise," I said, though I was beginning to have my doubts.

"Isaac? What's he doing here with you? I thought you didn't like him."

Sitting back on the bed, I patted a place next to me.

"One thing at a time. I want to hear why *you're* here first," I said, wiping her teary face with my skirt hem.

"They put me in this room and locked the door," she said.

"They?"

"That man—Mr. Walton."

I stared in Peg's direction, appalled. "He did *what*? *Why*? You were seen getting on the Bristol coach. And you took your things, Peg. You were running away, and now Da's gone looking for you. How the heck did you end up here?"

"Mr. Walton said I had to stay out of the way, otherwise it would ruin the surprise for the guests."

"Whoa, slow down a bit." I wondered how much of Peg's story could be true. It already sounded very jumbled up. "How did you get here in the first place? *Were* you on that Bristol coach at all?"

"For a mile or two, yes. I sat next to a lady who was coming to stay at Eden Court. She was with her husband and stepsister and she asked where I was going. And I told her that I was running away."

"So why did you get off again?"

"I got scared, Lizzie. It was awful squashed on the coach, and when I thought of how crowded Bristol would be, I felt sick. I wished you were with me but you weren't, though the lady was nice and kind and . . ." She took a deep breath. "Then the coach stopped at Eden Court and Mr. Walton was waiting at the gates for the lady and her friends. He saw me and said I'd better come with him too."

So this lady, it seemed, was one of Mr. Walton's guests who Jeffers and the maid were running themselves ragged trying to serve. It didn't explain why Peg was in this cellar, though.

"Why did Mr. Walton want you here?"

"He said he needed me to help him with something. It sounded better than going to Bristol, at least for now."

I frowned. "And you *went* with him? The man's a stranger, Peg."

"Da said he was a genius," Peg retorted.

I sighed. She was right: Da had said that. And look where it had got us.

"Why the cellar?" I still didn't understand this part.

"Mr. Walton said he had to hide me away. He didn't want the guests to see any more of me, otherwise I'd completely ruin the treat he had in store for them. He called me the lightning girl, Lizzie. What d'you think he meant?"

I shook my head. "I don't know."

Yet hearing her say those words turned me icy cold. Mr. Walton had used that very phrase before, on the night my geese went missing. And the woman with him had said Peg taking the blame was "a considerable inconvenience." I didn't understand what it meant—what any of it meant. But it was clear they wanted Peg for a special reason, and that reason was to do with lightning.

I knew I'd been right not to trust Mr. Walton. He wasn't a genius, despite what Da said. He was a sinister man who cared for nothing but science. And here we now were, trapped at Eden Court with him and some strange, howling creature.

Unable to sit still any longer, I swung my legs off the bed and stood up. It was no good waiting for Isaac to rescue us when it was obvious he wasn't returning. My sense was he'd got scared and done a flit to the village. Or he'd just forgotten me. Either way, it was down to us: we'd have to rescue ourselves.

"Right, Peg, where's the main door?"

We reached it in four short steps. It was locked.

"We really are stuck, aren't we?" said Peg, a wobble in her voice.

"Let me think a minute. I'll come up with something, I

promise." Yet all I could picture were tombs and graveyards: if no one ever came for us, we'd be as good as buried alive.

In my agitation I paced up and down, trailing my hands along the wall. The stone was rough. Crumbly with damp. Just by the bed was an odd, smooth spot. When I knocked against it, the sound was hollow.

"Shh!" I said to Peg, though she wasn't making any noise. "Listen to this."

I knocked again.

"Is it a cupboard?" asked Peg. "Because I can't see a handle."

I couldn't feel one either. On pressing against it, I heard the click of a catch.

"It's another little door!" cried Peg. She knelt down beside me, holding the rushlight before her. "It doesn't look like a cupboard inside either, because there's no back to it."

"Is it a tunnel?"

"I think so," said Peg.

"Thank goodness!" I gasped.

Then the doubts came back.

"Did Mr. Walton mention it?" I asked, wondering if it was a trap he'd set and he'd be waiting for us at the other end.

"No, though he did say this was the best place to hide me. Said I'd never escape, so there was no point trying."

Another of Mr. Walton's slip-ups, then: he was starting to chalk them up. If this was our only chance to get out, we had to take it.

Chapter 19

BEING IN THE TUNNEL WASN'T too bad at first. It was so narrow I could touch the walls on either side without even stretching out my arms, but knowing there was an open door behind us helped me stay calm. Then, twenty yards or so in, we seemed to drop down further. The air grew colder. Peg's light guttered furiously.

"Careful, there's another step," said Peg, slowing her pace. Then, a few yards on, "The tunnel goes sharp right here."

I almost wished she hadn't said so, for once we'd turned the corner that door was no longer behind us and the walls seemed to close in just that bit more. The damp smell grew so I could almost taste it. Cobwebs tickled my cheeks. The air was so thick it caught in my throat. Something darted over my foot. I felt another vermin-sized body brush past my ankle. Just ahead of me, Peg gave a loud gasp.

"Rats! They're big ones, Lizzie."

I hesitated. Rats had never bothered me, not like they did Mercy, who'd squeal at the sight of one. This was different. I couldn't tell where they were, not until they touched me. It made me want to run—though run *where*? It was either back to the cellar or keep going. Suddenly neither seemed much of an option.

"Don't stop. Keep moving," I said. "Wave your light at them if they come too close."

Poor Peg did her best. In one hand she held her rushlight aloft. In the other, she gripped my fingers so hard they went numb. Step by step we inched along the tunnel.

"They're as big as cats!" Peg said.

"Don't be silly," I said. "How *can* they be?"

Peg lunged forward. "Get back!" she cried, waving the light in front of her with such force it went out.

Something muscular squirmed past my leg.

"It came up to my knee! I swear it did!" I cried.

As Peg took off in panic, I was right behind. The darkness didn't matter, nor that we'd no idea where we were heading. All we cared about was running. Away from the rats. Away from the cellar. Away from Mr. Walton.

We kept going for what felt like miles. Upwards, downwards. The damp-smelling tunnel seemed never-ending. And then, quite suddenly the air grew warmer. The darkness turned a murky gray.

"Is that a door up ahead?" I asked, panting for breath.

"Think so. It's got light round its edges."

As we got closer, Peg was all for bursting straight through the door, but I held her back.

"Wait a second," I whispered. "We don't know where it goes. We don't want to rush out and get caught, do we?"

Mr. Walton probably had an office or a library or something, and it would be just our luck that this door opened straight into it. An hour or so ago this might've been helpful. But Da's note wasn't important anymore. What mattered was getting Peg out of here, away from whatever Mr. Walton was planning to do with her.

135

"Let me listen at the door." Gesturing for Peg to step aside, I pressed my ear against the wood. All I heard was silence. And Peg breathing heavily at my shoulder.

"I can't hear anything over you huffing and puffing," I said.

She drew a single, sharp breath. Something was scuttling towards us. I heard rustling. Scratching. Peg flung her arms around my waist.

"Oh, Lizzie!" she squealed. "It's those rats again! Loads of them!"

"Shh! Keep quiet."

Pressing her face into my frock she started to sob. Something terrifyingly large lumbered across my feet. Another brushed against my ankles. Then a surge of fur and muscle writhed past our legs.

"There's so many!" I gasped in horror.

Peg's sobs fast became wails, echoing off the tunnel. All the while, I tried to tell her to shush, that it would be all right, but I sensed something scampering vertically up the wall just inches from my face. Close enough to feel a flick of tail against my chin. To hear the skitter of claws. And when my hair began to move and I felt whiskers tickle my ear, I panicked.

With all my might, I flew at the door. It gave way against my shoulder. The force sent me stumbling out into daylight, Peg still hugging my waist. I kicked the door shut behind us. Then, loosening Peg's grip, I took a lungful of air. Beat by beat, my heart began to slow. I still couldn't hear anyone. The room, or wherever we were, felt empty. It smelled strange too, of something I couldn't name. It was strong enough to make my nose tingle.

"Where are we?" I whispered.

"Don't know," said Peg. "It's got shelves on the walls like a library, but . . ."

"But what?"

"They aren't books on the shelves. They're jars with things in them, like when we pickle vegetables for winter, only these things, well . . ." She paused. "They aren't vegetables either."

"What are they?" Though, from her shocked tones, I wasn't sure I wanted to know.

Peg hugged me tight. "Oh, Lizzie! They're queer, horrible things, like baby animals and birds and toads with two heads!"

What I'd suspected in that cage outside was bad enough. But this filled me with a new disgust. In that single moment, I was almost glad I couldn't see the shelves, though it all bloomed inside my head anyway: jars of dark fluid and floating inside them, little, fishlike bodies, their white flesh pressed against the glass.

"Let's get out of here," I said, prying Peg off me and taking her hand. "But please, not back through that tunnel."

"There's another door. We'll go that way," said Peg.

I nodded. If it took us out into a hall then we'd creep along it, silent as mice. Before we'd even reached the door, it opened.

". . . for goodness' sake! Put her in a bedroom, not a cellar! We want the child alive and well, not sick with fever, or worse," said a woman, clearly scolding someone. "It's what our guests have come to see. And if the weather *is* turning and we get a storm tonight, then . . ."

Two sets of footsteps came to a halt in front of us.

"Oh! Gracious!" the woman cried.

The other voice was Mr. Walton's. "What on earth? How did *you* get in here?"

Making sure Peg was tucked safely behind me, I stood tall. I was seething. And terrified. Though I didn't want him to see it.

"We're going home, Mr. Walton. Our da's been worried sick about where Peg's been," I said.

"Can't keep that nose of yours out of anything, can you?" he cried.

"She doesn't wish to stay and be part of your 'surprise.' She's proper upset, she is. But luckily for her, you hid her in a cellar with a secret passage connected to it, so we got out just in time."

"What nonsense! That cellar was perfectly secure." But I could hear him flustering.

"If you'll excuse us," I said. "Come on, Peg."

As I went to walk past him his hand shot out and grabbed my upper arm, pinching the skin between his fingers.

"Release your sister at once!" Mr. Walton said.

"Get off me!" Pulling back, I twisted and squirmed whilst desperately trying to hold on to Peg.

"Stop this minute! All of you!" cried the woman.

She spoke with such authority, I knew at once she was the same person who'd been with Mr. Walton that night on Mill Lane.

"Let go of both girls this instant," she said.

Tutting angrily, Mr. Walton shoved us away from him. I put my arm around Peg's shoulders. Whoever this woman was, *she* was the person giving orders to him, not the other way round. And now she'd saved us from his clutches. I reckoned I owed her a thank-you.

I cleared my throat. "Miss . . ."

"Stine. Francesca Stine."

She must've moved, for I caught a waft of her scent. It was the same as this room's, chemical and eye-wateringly strong.

"Miss, I'm taking my sister home," I said. "I don't know what Mr. Walton was planning to do with Peg, but we aren't staying to find out. My poor da's beside himself with worry, so the sooner we get home, the better."

I half expected a gasp of horror. A sympathetic cry. Maybe even a call to bring the carriage round to the front and drive us back to Sweepfield.

Instead, Miss Stine said, "Peg? Did you just call your sister *Peg*?"

I frowned. "That's her name."

She made an irritable sound in her throat. Her skirts swished as she turned away from us then back again.

"You idiot!" Her voice was a low, furious rumble. "You absolute, incompetent idiot!"

My mouth fell open. "There's no need to call me—"

"Not you!" she spat. *"Him!"*

Mr. Walton, who'd gone eerily quiet, drew a breath as if he was about to explain himself. I'd still no real idea what this was concerning. But I had second thoughts about thanking anyone now.

"Excuse us," I said. "We're leaving."

We managed two steps before Miss Stine took hold of my wrist.

"Not so fast," she said. "I told Mr. Walton to bring me Lizzie Appleby—the famous lightning child. Can you believe it? All this effort, all this secrecy. And the idiot brought me the wrong girl!"

Chapter 20

"N-NO, MISS, YOU'RE MISTAKEN," I stuttered.

Even so, I directed Peg to stand safely behind me again.

"I'm not mistaken," Miss Stine said. "Since being in Sweepfield, I've heard your story and it interests me greatly."

This might've been a compliment for some people. Yet to me, who'd endured more than my fair share of being pointed at and talked about, it made my heart sink.

"I'm someone who lost her mam and her eyesight. That's my *story*," I said bitterly.

"But I'd no idea *this* girl was blind!" Mr. Walton cut in. I sensed he was pointing at me. "She wanders the streets at night, snoops about up here. And she looks right at me when I speak. It's the other girl, the little one who seized our other specimen, that *I* thought—"

"Save your excuses," Miss Stine interrupted him. "Lizzie, how would you like to stay at Eden Court for a few days to help me in my work?" She sounded excited.

"What, *here*?"

"Yes."

I was aware of Peg clinging to my dress. On my left, Miss

Stine's cool fingers circled my wrist. And behind us those jars of deformed creatures, and Mr. Walton breathing short, impatient breaths through his nose.

"No, miss," I said. "We must get home."

Her grip on my wrist tightened. "So must I, Lizzie. I'm needed back in London, but I'm staying on at Eden Court solely to find out more about what happened to you in that lightning storm. So you really must help me. My future ambitions could depend on it."

"You want to find out . . . about *me*?" I didn't much want to think about that day. And I certainly didn't want to talk about it to a stranger.

Yet there was something about the way she asked. She was showing an interest in me—not in a whispering-behind-hands kind of way, but because she wanted to hear the truth.

"Yes," Miss Stine said. "I'm a scientist, an anatomist. I study how the human body works, and recently I've become very interested in electricity. You'll see how important you are to my work soon enough."

My mouth dropped. "So *you're* the scientist?"

All this time I'd been certain it was Mr. Walton. So had most of Sweepfield.

"How can that be, Miss Stine?" Peg sounded as confused as I felt. "You're a . . . umm . . . well . . . a *girl*."

Miss Stine gave a little laugh. "I'm a bit older than a girl, but you're right, this work is mostly done by men. It's made things hard for me. People see a person in skirts and—*whoosh*—they make assumptions about how I should be. Never mind that I might be on the brink of an amazing discovery. What matters most is how I look."

I nodded: I knew what that felt like.

"It's why I hide myself away most of the time," said Miss Stine. "But don't be afraid, Lizzie. You'll be safe here."

"What about him, though?" I nodded in the direction of Mr. Walton. "He had our Peg locked up in a cellar."

"I told him to keep her hidden, but I'd had no idea he'd put her down there. I can only apologize." She sounded suitably ashamed. "Mr. Walton, my assistant, was a little overenthusiastic in his duties yesterday. He will follow orders more closely from now on."

Mr. Walton coughed uncomfortably. Despite his expensive voice and smart clothes, he was, in fact, a servant. It wasn't him who had rented Eden Court, but Miss Stine, and it made me braver somehow, because whatever threats he'd made, he wasn't lord and master after all.

Yet still I couldn't shake off the sense that something wasn't right. If Mr. Walton was working *for* Miss Stine, then how nasty did that make her? And this troubled me the most, because she didn't seem very nasty at all.

"We really can't stay, miss," I said. "Da will wonder where we've got to." Which wasn't true; he'd be in Bristol by now, and the lie made me flush.

"We'll send word to your father. Peg can take a message."

At this, Peg buried her face in my ribs. "I'm not going anywhere without you, Lizzie!"

"Come now, no tears," Miss Stine said.

"Hush, Peg," I said, trying desperately to think of a solution. If only Isaac hadn't disappeared, then he could've taken her to Mercy's.

"I won't go back to Sweepfield on my own," Peg insisted.

"Everyone there hates me. If you try to send me, I swear I'll run away again!"

Which was no sort of answer. I think Miss Stine realized it too.

"I know!" she said, as if the idea surprised her. "Why don't you both stay? It could be of great help. You'll be perfectly safe."

It was the second time she'd mentioned our safety.

"You promise?" I said.

"Absolutely. Have no fear."

She'd shifted position a little so the light was behind her, which meant I could just about see her outline. She was small for a grown-up—not much taller than Mercy.

"You want to *study* me?" I asked again.

"Exactly. I am on the brink of a discovery so"—she searched for the word—"*incredible,* it will change the course of science, of HISTORY! Wouldn't you like to be part of that with me, Lizzie? Wouldn't you like to be FAMOUS?"

Behind us, Mr. Walton shuffled his feet. My stomach did a nervous clench.

"I don't fancy it much, to be honest," I muttered.

All I'd ever wanted from life was to work hard and keep geese and eat supper each night at a table with those I loved. Yet how could I explain it to someone like her, who wanted so much more?

I took a deep breath and tried.

"I don't want any more attention, miss. I don't want people always pointing at me in the street. I just want to *be,* like I was before . . ." I couldn't say the rest. Not the words "accident" or "lightning strike" or "blindness," or "my mother dead in the snow." In my mouth they'd turned to dust.

"Lizzie, your life *has* changed. It won't ever be the same, so it's pointless to wish for it."

"But—" I tried to protest.

"What I'm working towards is something miraculous," she insisted. "Something so ambitious that one day it will save the lives of our loved ones. Or perhaps even bring back those who've already died."

"Oh . . . goodness . . ."

Was she serious? Could science *do* that?

It was a stunning and completely terrifying idea, and for a moment my head went dizzy. Then I remembered what Da had said about Mr. Walton's work. He'd called him a genius and said one day he'd be famous the world over. Which must mean Da didn't know of Miss Stine's existence. But for that night on Mill Lane, she really had stayed hidden away, doing her work in secret.

"The world doesn't care for female scientists, you know," Miss Stine said. "My research could change all that forever. It could prove that women are just as intelligent, just as hungry to achieve as men. We wouldn't be solely wives and mothers and sisters and daughters. *Our* names would be on statues, on monuments, written in the history books. Think of *that*, Lizzie."

It sounded incredible. And the way she seemed willing to share all this made me feel important, like I was to be trusted with her biggest, wildest dreams.

"But my da won't like us being here," I said, unsure what else to say. "He told me to come straight home."

"Don't fret. I'll pay very handsomely for your time," Miss Stine replied.

It was getting harder to refuse. With this cold, wet spring there was already talk of crops failing and food prices rising. In addition to finding Peg safe and sound, Da would be pleased if we earned a bit of coin.

"You'll be working for me just as your father does making my workbench, though he believes it's for Mr. Walton, which keeps things simpler," Miss Stine added. "So what do you think? *Do* say yes."

The sensible thing would be to say no and go home. Yet still I dithered. These past few minutes Miss Stine had spoken to me as if I was someone worth knowing. Something had shifted, as if a fast-asleep part of me had woken up at last.

"Oh, and, Lizzie," Miss Stine said before I had a chance to speak. "We have other guests too—important people from London with modern ideas like mine. They're traveling to Switzerland and have stopped in on their way. I want you to meet them tomorrow."

I gulped. "Oh . . . I mean . . . gosh." A thrill of excitement ran through me.

"So, will you accept my invitation to stay? Will you two also be my guests?" she asked.

"Yes," I said, trying not to grin. "Yes, all right."

Though it didn't seem I had much choice in the matter: she still had hold of my wrist.

A maid called Ruth was summoned to escort us to a bedchamber upstairs.

"Miss Stine's put you in a room at the top of the house," she said. It was the same woman who'd earlier answered the front door to me. "A smart room it is too," she added with a sniff.

"What's eating her?" Peg whispered as we followed her up countless flights of stairs. "She looks awful grim."

I prodded Peg for being cheeky. "She's busy with those London guests and now she's got lumped with us, that's what."

At the very top of the stairs, we went through a door, then along a twisty passage and down a single step that nearly sent me flying. At last, we reached our room.

"This is yours," said Ruth, opening the door. "Though why you're still here, I don't know. You should've gone home when you could."

I wanted to ask what she meant. But by now Peg had pushed her way past us both and was squealing in delight at our bedchamber. Ruth left without a by-your-leave.

Not knowing what to make of it all, I hovered in the doorway. Perhaps we should go home. It wasn't too late to change our minds.

Yet inside the room Peg grew ever louder. She was laughing too, and sounding so joyous that despite my doubts, I couldn't help but smile. "What is it, Peg? What can you see?"

"It's wonderful!" she cried, pulling me across the threshold. "It's the grandest bedchamber I've EVER known. And it's all ours!"

I laughed. "For a night or two, maybe. Don't get too used to it, mind."

Yet I sensed Peg was right: the room was beautiful. Even the air felt soft and warm and expensive. Any doubts I had began to melt away.

"The bed is VAST, Lizzie! It's got curtains draped around it, and the bedsheets are so white, and the pillows soft feather ones. . . ." She let go of me and crossed the room. "Oh! You can see all sorts out this window."

"Like what?"

"The driveway, stables, trees . . ."

As she prattled on I heard the joy in her voice, and it made me smile more. "'Tis better than that cellar, anyhow."

"Oh, it really is!" Peg gasped. "There's a jar of biscuits by the bed, and a roaring fire, and they've even left us fresh nightgowns to wear."

It sounded almost too good to be true.

Kicking off my boots and stockings, I walked barefoot across the carpet towards where patches of gray light indicated the windows. One sash was raised a little, the air coming in smelling damp, as if rain was on the way. I leant my elbows on the sill and breathed deep. Ruth was probably exaggerating, I decided, or irritable and tired. Miss Stine had been polite and charming, and she was oh so clever to be doing such important work. I'd never met a real scientist before, especially not a lady one. And the way she'd spoken, promising things I'd not thought possible, made my own mind flare up like a piece of just-struck tinder. It was impossible not to be intrigued. Anyway, we'd only be here a few days—and kept in the height of luxury too. I'd be mad not to enjoy myself.

The floor creaked as Peg came to join me at the window.

"Lizzie," she said, sounding serious. "I hope Spider's all right without us."

"He'll be fine. Our house isn't fancy like this place, and that's good if you're a cat, because there's plenty he can catch and eat."

"Like spiders," Peg agreed.

"And flies."

"And mice."

"And the pie Mercy brought this morning . . ."

A noise drifted in through the open window. The sound made my blood chill.

Peg heard it too. "What was *that?*"

I didn't answer; I didn't know how to.

It was the howl of the wild animal. And a reminder: not all guests here at Eden Court were of the human kind.

Chapter 21

AS NIGHT DREW IN, RAIN began to fall—soft and whispery at first, then a steady, relentless drumming on the rooftops. A different maid brought us supper, laying a table near the fire and filling it with many dishes; Peg took great delight in explaining each one. There were pastries and meat in rich, creamy sauces, fresh-baked bread, slices of pear, shortbread, lemon posset still warm with a thick froth on top.

"It's a supper fit for two princesses!" she cried.

"Well, we *are* important guests, remember?" I told her, as if anyone could forget it in a bedchamber so richly carpeted and warm.

Though Peg tucked into supper as if it were the last meal she'd ever have, I was too excited to eat much of it. Afterwards, with nothing else to do but sleep, we crawled into bed. Peg started snoring almost straight away. But I lay listening to all the unfamiliar sounds. Outside, rain rattled against the windows. The wind had picked up too, moaning and whistling round the chimneys. Somewhere deep inside the house, a door opened, then closed. Pulling the blankets round my shoulders, I attempted to go to sleep. But my eyes kept springing open. The more I tried, the harder it became.

Then.

Something was outside our window.

I sat up sharply. Straining my ears, I heard footsteps—someone was on the driveway. My head filled with visions of Da come to take us home. Or Mercy. Or perhaps even Isaac. Part of me felt very glad. Another part wasn't sure I wanted to leave just yet, not when we were being treated so well and there were exciting guests from London to meet.

I leapt out of bed. But the window wasn't where I remembered, and I walked straight into a chair. The pain of it cleared any last traces of sleep from my head. Of course it couldn't be Da outside. He was miles away in Bristol, searching for his daughter who all the time was here with me. And I couldn't tell him or reach him because I was too busy enjoying myself as Miss Stine's guest, and I felt a horrible pang of guilt.

Gradually, I sensed a line of gray in the dark. This must be the window with the curtains almost closed; it wouldn't hurt to check who was out there. The window was still open, the sill wet with rainwater. From directly underneath, the sounds of conversation wafted upwards. The speakers were men. Though they were trying to keep quiet their rage was obvious in their tight, spitting voices. My shoulders tensed as I listened.

"Who was the last to feed it?" This was Mr. Walton.

"Me, s'morning when that lad from the village brought the pig carcass. Jeffers said he had too much else to do," said a gruff voice. Perhaps this was the man who'd spotted Isaac and me down that path where we shouldn't have been. He didn't sound very kindly. If it was him then I hoped Isaac had given him the slip.

"You'll recall how it got out two nights ago. And how we only just managed to recapture it?"

"Yes, sir."

"The locals are talking, Mr. Cox. We cannot allow this to keep happening. I trust you double-checked the pen?"

"We did."

"And you filled in those holes by the fence?"

"Yes, sir. With rocks."

"Then how the devil has it escaped this time?"

"It got out through the gate," said the gruff man who was clearly Mr. Cox.

"The gate? The GATE?"

Next came the thud of a fist hitting flesh. I winced. "What do we pay you for, eh?" By now, Mr. Walton was almost screaming. "Slack, that's what you are! Utterly slack!"

His shouting made me nervous. Today he'd been the one making mistakes, and now the tables had turned. This was about more than an escaped animal. It was about his own humiliation. And like all bullies, he had to inflict it on someone else.

As quickly as it had started, the arguing stopped. Something was being passed between the two men.

"You've used a rifle before, have you, Mr. Cox?" Mr. Walton asked.

A rifle?

I gripped the windowsill. So far the animal had killed only livestock. But what if it was capable of attacking something bigger? A *person*?

"We used muskets in the army," Mr. Cox replied, gruffer than ever after being walloped.

"Right. Take these."

A metallic click. A clunk. The shuffling of limbs.

"These rifles are more accurate than a musket. Only fire if you can see the beast clearly. We don't want to waste shot."

Or injure the creature, I thought grimly. For though it had killed my geese, I couldn't help but feel sorry for it. Shut in its pen, it'd sounded so sad, as if it were already dying a slow, painful death. At least, I supposed, if it did get shot, it would be spared more of that misery.

The men moved on. Their footsteps grew faint. All I could hear now was the rain.

Then came another noise from behind me. It was the click of a door opening. I turned round. Held my breath. In the darkness, a candle flickered.

"Come! Quickly now!" The speaker was Miss Stine. "My London guests are waiting downstairs to meet you. We've not got much time!"

I'd no idea who I expected it to be. But at the sound of her voice I almost laughed with relief. Then I grew confused.

"It's the middle of the night, miss. You said I'd meet them tomorrow."

"Yes, and you'll have heard the rain—there's a storm just beginning. If we're very lucky I might be able to try something out."

I felt suddenly flustered. I wasn't ready to meet anyone. Not at night. Not if it meant leaving Peg behind. And I certainly didn't want to sit through a storm, not with strangers.

Miss Stine must've seen this in my face, for she took my hand. "My dear, you're trembling."

"I'm a bit cold, that's all," I said, trying to sound brave.

"Then you must wear this over your nightgown." She draped something light and warm over my shoulders. "There. Is that better?"

It felt like a shawl or a blanket of the softest wool. Once again, I had that sense of being cared for. All I had to do was enjoy these lavish attentions. It really wasn't *that* hard.

"Yes, miss. Thank you."

"Right," Miss Stine said, linking her arm through mine like Mercy would, only more firmly. "Let's go, shall we?"

She didn't mean it as a question, but it seemed polite to nod.

"Good. The guests cannot wait to meet you, Lizzie. Isn't this so *very* thrilling?"

She certainly made it sound so. I'd never imagined people from London ever wanting to meet *me*.

Yet a little niggle at the back of my brain told me to be wary. For all its luxury, Eden Court was still a peculiar place. There were men outside with guns, for starters. Not to mention that room downstairs with its shelves full of jars. This was a conversation for later, I decided. Right now the London guests were expecting us.

And we were, it seemed, in a hurry.

Miss Stine whisked me down the staircase in a flash. We hit the hallway at speed, our feet sliding over the marble floor as if it were ice. Then along a corridor that smelled of beeswax. Down steps. Round a corner. Breathless, we went through a door.

It opened onto a room full of candlelight and voices. The conversation fizzled as we entered. Someone came towards us.

"Ah, Francesca." It wasn't Mr. Walton. This man spoke in the same expensive way but sounded softer somehow. "We've been discussing our plans. We're in rather a rush to get to the coast, as you know. We've a boat to catch and would rather not loiter, especially with a storm on the way."

"Loiter?" Miss Stine said sharply. "Percy, you're too late. The storm is already upon us. So please, resume your seat."

"Oh. Right. Well, if you say so." The man backed away.

A chair was pulled up for me; Miss Stine's hands on my shoulders guided me into it. I sat, heart thumping, to face strangers

I couldn't see. Yet I knew they were looking: their gazes made me flush. And bizarre though it was, I felt almost glad, as if I was being noticed not as a freak but because of who I was.

"Dear friends," Miss Stine said, all charm again. "May I introduce our guest of honor tonight, Lizzie Appleby."

Sensing her hands leave my shoulders, I sat taller in my seat. A smattering of applause made me flush even more. My mouth twitched into a smile.

"I had promised you'd meet her tomorrow," Miss Stine continued. "You were to see her scars and hear her remarkable story—this would be astonishing enough. But . . ." She paused dramatically. "You'll notice how the weather has deteriorated this evening. There is a storm building, so I've called you to the drawing room to meet Lizzie tonight because I want to try something out."

The guests clapped politely. Part of me was dying to know what Miss Stine had planned; the other part soaked up the applause as if it were some rich, sweet treat I didn't want to end.

"Lizzie," Miss Stine said, speaking over my head. "May I introduce you to Mr. Percy Shelley, a poet, his . . . *companion*, Miss Mary Godwin, and her sister . . ."

"Stepsister," a woman interrupted. "We share a father through marriage, that's all."

"Apologies, *step*sister, Miss Claire Clairmont."

Their names meant nothing, not then. It was just something more to add to the giddiness in my brain.

"Now, if we could darken the room ready for my demonstration," Miss Stine said.

There were sounds of movement as candle flames were pinched. The bright places became shadows. I tried to ask what was going on, but no one answered me. Within moments, the preparations were done. As the guests resumed their seats, the air in the room grew thick and still. Outside, though, the wind was gusting again.

"You are well aware of my interest in electricity," Miss Stine began. "Imagine my total joy, then, to discover Lizzie Appleby here in the village of Sweepfield. You see, Lizzie has been struck by a lightning bolt and survived. Tonight we will—"

"Miss, I'm not sure I'm ready," I blurted out, suddenly uncertain. The mere mention of lightning made me tremble.

"Don't fret," she said under her breath. "I promise you'll come to no harm."

Three times now she'd mentioned my safety. And though it should've comforted me, like the shawl and the fancy supper, it didn't.

"I don't mean to seem ungrateful for your kindness, miss, but—"

"Just sit still!" Irritation crept into her voice. "Now, as I was saying, tonight we will consider the effects of lightning on the human body."

"On Lizzie," Mr. Shelley cut in.

Miss Stine gave a short-tempered sigh. She really didn't like being interrupted. "As a scientist, I prefer to think of the anatomy, the human body rather than the person," she said.

"But—"

"Percy, please," Miss Stine said. "This is science. What I'm on the verge of discovering is astonishing. Life-changing. So let's not be sentimental. In the pursuit of progress we often have to make difficult decisions, and to consider the more *far-reaching* consequences of our actions. This time, I believe, I've got it right."

Which made it sound as if she'd once got something wrong.

Chapter 22

"WHAT IS THE ESSENCE OF life? What turns us from lifeless matter into animated beings?"

Outside, the rain kept pouring, blown hard against the windows. In contrast, the room was strangely quiet. Miss Stine held everyone's attention. I imagined the guests on the edge of their seats as I sat uneasily in mine.

"What is the force that animates us?" Miss Stine went on. "What makes our muscles move, our eyes open, our lungs breathe in and out?"

No one answered.

"We don't know," Miss Stine said. "Nor does the Royal College of Surgeons know—though that charlatan Dr. Lawrence thinks he does. Yes, Mary and Percy, I appreciate you think highly of him, but *I* believe the answer lies right here."

Her hand fell onto my shoulder. I flinched.

"W-with me?" I stuttered.

She kept talking. "On January twenty-third a freak thunderstorm descends on the village of Sweepfield. Two people rounding up cattle in a field are struck by lightning. One dies instantly, the other miraculously survives. Is it chance? Is it luck? Or is it something more complicated? Is it *electricity*?"

Miss Clairmont gasped, clearly thrilled. Yet I'd not expected Miss Stine to speak of Mam, and it threw me off balance. This was my story, mine and Mam's. The way Miss Stine told it made it sound so dramatic, so awful, I almost believed it had happened to someone else.

"The victim died instantly, I'm told. The only marks to her body were on her fingertips, which were blackened and charred. Her boots were found twenty yards away: they had been blasted completely off her feet.

"Yet the survivor here"—she patted me—"was hit by the same bolt. Which must mean that as it traveled through another body, the lightning lost energy, making its second strike that bit less powerful."

Mr. Shelley cut in: "This is fascinating, but poor Lizzie is looking terribly pale. Perhaps less of the physical details?"

"Shh, Percy!" Miss Godwin said. "Francesca's an anatomist—of course we need to hear the physical details."

They might, but I didn't. It felt like someone had stamped on my chest.

Pressing my hands against my ears, I blocked out Miss Stine's voice until it became a hum. I stayed like that, until her tone softened. Then, hesitantly, I dropped my hands to my lap.

". . . so what I've learned is electricity can be weakened, and that there's a point where its force can be tolerated. Too much and it causes damage. Our specimen here *is* damaged."

I swallowed.

She was talking now about me. She'd pushed up my nightgown sleeve too, and though I should've sat still to be looked at like she wanted, I felt only toe-curling shame.

"No, please," I said, trying to pull my sleeve down again. "I'd really rather you didn't . . ."

She ignored my protests. "Observe the scars left by the lightning strike. Here at the elbow, and here at the shoulder and up to the neck and jaw. Come closer, do."

Chairs scraped against the floor as people stood up. I felt them crowd around me. Heard their "oohs" and "hmms" and "my goodnesses." I wished they'd stop, but I bore it because, despite myself, I still wanted to please Miss Stine.

"Now to my purpose," Miss Stine said. "We know of the exciting developments already made in this field—Galvani's work on making frogs' legs twitch and Volta's on how electric currents pass from one form to another. And we've all heard of the experiments done on dead bodies—on murderers fresh from the gallows."

"I haven't." The voice was young, girlish—Miss Clairmont's. "Though I'm not sure I wish to."

I didn't either. Yet I felt compelled to listen.

"These discoveries all point to electricity as a life force, a property of life." Miss Stine spoke quickly. "It is quite dizzyingly simple. A single potent energy that bestows life upon dead matter. Imagine what we could do with this knowledge! Imagine the power it might give us!"

"Would it be possible, do you think, to bring the dead back to life?" Miss Godwin asked, her voice husky with emotion.

"I believe it is. We only need to fathom how much or how little electricity is required. And then, who knows?"

The room fell silent. Miss Godwin was the first to speak, in barely a whisper. "This is incredible. If what you say is true, we'd need never lose anyone to death ever again."

It dawned on me what she meant. Everything died. *Everyone* died. That was life. It was as plain as the leaves on the trees.

And yet.

There were stupider things to believe in—in Pilgrim's Meadow on Midwinter's Eve there'd been superstitions aplenty. If scientists found a way to bring back to life people who'd died, well, Miss Godwin was right. It would be incredible.

Yet none of what'd been said sank in; I wouldn't let it. Just thinking of Mam alive again was so wonderful, so joyous, it was agony.

Miss Godwin, though, grew animated. "Imagine it, Percy. Our own dear daughter brought back to life. And my mother, sat here amongst us right now."

It couldn't actually *work*, could it? Twitching frogs' legs were one thing, but to revive a whole human being was something else entirely.

"Mary, my love." Mr. Shelley tried to calm Miss Godwin. "This is a dangerous gift we speak of. People don't take kindly to challenges on creation. It's seen as us humans trying to be godlike."

"If it could spare our daughter from the grave, then I'll gladly be godlike," Miss Godwin retorted.

"Perhaps, and it is intriguing, but—"

"I want to know more," Miss Godwin interrupted. There were rustlings as she took her seat again. She was a force to be reckoned with, this Miss Godwin. I didn't know if I liked her or feared her. "Francesca, please, continue."

Mr. Shelley, tutting, sat down.

Something had changed. The room felt different. The *air* felt different, thrumming with excitement and expectation, and I couldn't help but be swept along with it. Miss Stine cracked her knuckles in readiness.

From the direction of the windows came a sudden flash of light. The hairs on my arm rose.

"Is that lightning?" Miss Clairmont gasped.

Perhaps someone nodded, I didn't know. I felt my scalp tingle. And down my left side, my scar began to pulse. My fingers went hot, then cold. It was the strangest sensation.

"Great heavens! Look at Lizzie!" Mr. Shelley cried. "What's happening to her?"

The tingling got stronger. Strands of hair loose about my shoulders seemed to lift. I didn't know whether to laugh or scream.

Miss Stine clapped in a sort of manic delight. "Yes! This is better than I'd hoped! She has an affinity with electricity, don't you see? Her previous lightning injuries make her the perfect specimen for my experiment!"

"Experiment?" The word pulled me up sharp.

"That's right," Miss Stine said. "That's why you're here."

"But . . ." I felt dazed. "I thought you liked me. I thought you wanted to talk to me and make notes about me, and . . ." Hearing how pitiful I sounded, I stopped.

The cold realization was I'd been duped.

"Don't make a fuss. The storm's almost here and we need to act fast," Miss Stine said.

I rose from the chair. Or tried to. Whip-quick, her hands were on my shoulders again, pushing me back into my seat.

"I'm an anatomist, Lizzie," she said through gritted teeth. "This isn't about you, not personally. It's about bodies and organs and blood and bone."

In that moment I saw what I was to her. The fine room, the rich supper, the kind words were all just a pretense. Really, I was just another two-headed creature in a jar. Or perhaps I was like that poor wild beast being hunted with guns this very minute. All Miss Stine wanted was another body to investigate.

She didn't seem to care if it was living or dead. It was there in her voice; underneath those rich person's manners she was as hard as flint. And I was blood and bone.

Hot, furious tears sprang to my eyes. How stupid I'd been to trust her. I wouldn't stay a moment longer. But again, as I tried to stand, she pushed me down. My legs buckled and I sat with a bump.

"Keep still!" she snapped, then to the others, "If lightning strikes the pole on the roof, it'll travel down through these copper wires." She must've pointed to something or held the wires up, for the guests all gasped. "We'll channel it as our source of electricity. Quickly, we must work fast!"

The room became a whirl of footsteps and bewildering sounds: clinkings and snappings and the dripping of water. Lightning flashed once. Twice. The thunder came just a beat after.

"Hurry!" Miss Stine cried. "The storm is almost directly overhead. If lightning strikes now, it should hit the roof pole."

I remembered what Mercy had seen on the roof, and how she'd mistaken it for a flagpole.

"What are you going to do to me?" I asked, hearing the trembling in my voice.

"I plan to re-create that moment you were struck, to see how much electricity you can tolerate."

My heart seemed to rise up into my throat. It stuck there, beating hard and very fast.

"No," I said. "You can't."

Her aim was for me to be hit by lightning. To see if I survived it.

Again.

I felt a throb of terror so strong I almost passed out.

"No," I gasped. "Please, no! You must let me go!"

But Miss Stine called for someone to help her and more hands seized me, pulling my arms behind my back. I twisted. Shouted. Kicked out with my feet. I was no match for two, maybe three sets of hands. They yanked me and turned me, till I was sure my arms would be torn from their sockets.

"Tie her fast! Make sure she can't escape," said Miss Stine.

Something tightened round my wrists. As I pulled against it, it dug into my flesh.

And then it was done. They'd tied me to the chair.

Try as I might, I couldn't move.

"This isn't fair!" I cried. "You can't keep me here like a prisoner!"

"Is there really any need to tie her so tightly?" Mr. Shelley asked.

"Indeed there is—look how she rages!" said Miss Stine. "I don't want to make a mistake."

This was all *so* wrong.

"Get off me! You shan't do this!" I yelled.

The more I fought, the more determined she was.

"Hold still, you little wretch!" she spat as someone rubbed vigorously at my temples, my neck, the soles of my feet.

"No!" I cried. "No!"

There was a clicking noise. She pressed cold metal against those places on my head, neck and feet. Wires crisscrossed my face.

Then, with a deep breath, she stood back.

"The equipment is in place. I believe we're ready." Her voice was icy calm as thunder roared overhead. "On the count of three ..."

I clenched my teeth. This was it. I braced myself for a

blinding blue flash. For that smell of burning and being blown out of my chair.

But there was no flash. Nor any lightning. Or if there was, nobody noticed, for the door flew open and Ruth the maid rushed in, unannounced and very flustered.

"Oh, miss! I've an urgent note! It's from her father. He's down in the village. Says he's looking for his daughter what's missing from home!"

Chapter 23

I GASPED OUT LOUD IN pure relief. So Da had returned from Bristol and, finding me not at home, had gone out in this terrible storm in search of me.

"You'd better untie these ropes," I said. "Because if my da comes here and sees what you're up to . . ."

Someone came and stood at my shoulder. The smell of cooking and beeswax polish told me it was Ruth.

"What the devil have they done to you, Lizzie?" she whispered under her breath.

I dreaded to think how things looked to her. If only I'd heeded her warning earlier. "What does my da say?" I cried. "Is he coming for me?"

"The note isn't for you," she whispered.

"What d'you mean? It must be."

"It's from Miss Godwin's father. She's . . ." Ruth paused. ". . . *run away* with Mr. Shelley, and Miss Clairmont's tagged along too. Mr. Godwin is furious. He's come to take her home before she brings shame on the family."

So it was someone else's father who wanted his daughter back. Not mine. Before I could help myself, the tears were back in my eyes.

Then, all at once, everyone seemed to be moving. Seats creaked, skirts rustled and Ruth was shooed out the door.

"We must leave immediately," Mr. Shelley said. "Mary, Claire, go upstairs and gather your things."

The experiment was forgotten. And instead of disappointment I felt suddenly ridiculously grateful to Miss Godwin's father, who by coming after his runaway daughter had saved me too.

Miss Godwin was not so thrilled. She hadn't forgotten the experiment either.

"But Francesca is all set to show us her idea. Can't we wait another hour?" she pleaded.

"No, we cannot," Mr. Shelley said. "If we leave now, we'll reach the coast by morning and catch an early sailing across the Channel."

Miss Clairmont joined in. "I agree with Percy. We should go now. The sooner we get to the Continent and to Switzerland, the better."

I could've hugged them both. *Go, then. Stop dithering.* This Switzerland place sounded a long way away. Hadn't they best get going?

"You always agree with Percy," Miss Godwin snapped. "Personally, I'm in no hurry to make a sea crossing in this foul weather. You know how sick I get."

"It'll be clear by morning," I said, though no one heard me.

"Well, I can't wait to see the Villa Diodati. It's got the most wonderful views of Lake Geneva, so I'm told. It's so kind of Lord Byron to invite us," said Miss Clairmont.

"He invited Percy and me, Claire," Miss Godwin said. "You chose to come along because you've nothing better to do."

I reckoned those two women could've bickered all night. Mr. Shelley, though, was keen to leave.

"Let's not dally," he begged.

"But I'm desperate to see if Francesca's idea really works," Miss Godwin said, close to tears. "Just think what could come from this, Percy. Our dear sweet Clara might never have had to die."

I held my breath, willing Mr. Shelley not to buckle. Hoping they'd all just go.

To my massive relief, he stood firm. "Your father's very angry, Mary. He wants his daughter back and he wants the money I promised him. But think of what *we* want, what we promised each other."

Miss Godwin sighed. I imagined her folding her arms like Mercy did when she was cross.

"To be free, to be different," she murmured. "Just as my mother was—yes, I know."

Then Miss Stine said, "Mary, Percy, listen. I've another idea. It's a little unusual, but it might go some way to helping with your grief over Clara. Come with me and I'll show you, though we'll need to be quick."

Almost as fast as I'd entered the room, the guests left it. But not before someone had untied my wrists and unhooked the wires from my head and body.

"Thank you," I said to I didn't know who.

Then the door closed and I was left alone, rubbing life back into my arms. I felt stunned. I wasn't even quite sure what had just happened, though I knew I'd had a lucky escape. Then I remembered Peg asleep upstairs.

We had to get away from this dreadful house. I'd been stupid enough to think we'd be safe here. I'd believed Miss Stine had a genuine interest in me. But vanity had dimmed my wits.

Everything at Eden Court felt dangerous.

Outside was a wild animal on the loose. Inside was Miss Stine, whose ambition made her as ruthless as that creature killing poultry. What she'd planned to do in this room was bad enough. I could only imagine what horrors went on in that other room, the one full of little bodies in jars. Instantly, my mind filled with images of limbs hacked off, of animal heads, and Miss Stine in a bloodstained apron like a butcher.

I stood up very slowly. The ground seemed to flex, then settle again. I walked until I found the nearest wall and felt along it for the door. I'd taken four or five steps, when, hearing voices, I stopped.

On the other side of the wall men were talking in a loud, boastful fashion.

"Did you see my shot, Mr. Walton? I picked him off clean, didn't I?"

"Indeed you did. You finished him completely. Bravo, my man."

The men were back from their hunt. And from the sound of it they'd killed the beast. As I pressed my ear to the wall, their voices out in the passageway grew clearer.

"Careful, don't drop him, Cox. She wants him as unspoiled as possible," Mr. Walton said.

"Bit late for that," the gruff man said.

They grunted and puffed as if they were carrying something heavy. Their boots tapped over the floor, growing fainter as they moved away.

Finally finding the door, I opened it just a crack. The passage was quiet now. Yet the creature's damp, woody smell still lingered.

Some way off another door creaked open.

"Good timing, Mr. Walton, Mr. Cox," said Miss Stine. "The

guests have just left for Switzerland—I don't think they were quite ready for my work after all. Bring him in, gently now."

"Don't you want us to bury him?" said Mr. Cox.

"Goodness, no!" Miss Stine said, and something else I didn't catch as the door closed behind them.

There was nothing more to hear but the crash of thunder. It was time to go. To find Peg and run. Yet no sooner was I feeling my way down the hallway than footsteps came up behind me.

"Sneaking off, are we?" Mr. Walton said.

I kept moving. "Peg and me are going home. You can't stop us."

Yet it seemed he could, as a hand clamped around my upper arm.

"Let go or I'll tell Miss Stine!" which was a stupid thing to say, but I prayed it might just throw him.

"Miss Stine? She sent me to fetch you, idiot girl!"

I wasn't about to give in. We grappled our way down the passage like a pair of fighting village boys, all arms and elbows and kicking feet. Once or twice I slipped in something wet. Something oily. I didn't want to think what it was.

Just at a point where the dark was at its darkest, Mr. Walton let me go.

"Enough!" he said, breathing heavily. "This is ridiculous, this fighting. What are we *doing*?"

I'd no intention of finding out.

"Wait, Miss Appleby," said Mr. Walton as I turned to run. "Please."

Something in his tone made me stop. He sounded odd. Almost broken.

"What is it? What d'you want?" I said.

He sighed. And it was a sad, sorry sound. "All my life I

168

wanted to make history. I had ambitions of my own, you see, to be the first man to explore the Arctic," he said. "Two years ago, I very nearly managed it. But the moment we hit pack ice, my men got scared and refused to sail on. I almost had a mutiny on my hands."

It was hard to hear him against the thunder, which still roared and grumbled outside. I didn't know why he was telling me these things either.

"You're not scared, though, are you, Miss Appleby? You have these injuries, yet you never give up. Perhaps I should've taken you with me—we might've made it then. And I'd be the brilliant one, employing people to assist *me*. As it stands, my ambitions are dead."

"I don't know about ambitions, Mr. Walton," I said.

"Really? Have you never wanted something *terribly*? Have you never started something risky and dangerous, and kept going because you wanted the glory that comes with the achievement?"

I didn't reply. Yet deep in my heart, I understood what he meant and pictured Mam chasing cattle in the snow. She had no intention of giving up that day. Though I loved her with a fierceness that would never die, she'd paid too high a price. So had I.

But I wasn't about to share such personal matters with Mr. Walton. And not with the lightning storm still flashing outside.

"I'm not hanging around so Miss Stine can fulfill her ambitions on me," I said. "Good night."

I took a step only to be yanked back again by my shawl.

"Not so fast, Miss Appleby. Miss Stine is still keen to convince you of the merits of her work. She wants you to witness a wonder of science."

He spun me so I was facing a different way. I felt dizzy. Disorientated. With my arms now pinned behind my back by his hand, I couldn't wriggle free. With his other hand, Mr. Walton rapped at what I guessed was a door—*rat-tat-tat-tat-tat-tat*—then waited. I caught snatches of conversation from inside.

"... a single shot to the neck ..."

"... considerable blood loss ..."

"... I don't believe ..."

Then Miss Stine, very firm. "You'll do as I say. Now, let's put him on the table." There came a grunt and a "One ... two ... three ... heave!" then the thud of something heavy being laid down.

I swallowed, for my mouth had gone dry. Mr. Walton, impatient, knocked again in the same six-beat way. Still no one came. Inside, I heard people moving about. Sighs, tuts, the lifting and putting down of more things.

"Enough of waiting," Mr. Walton muttered.

Swinging the door open, we went inside. The smell hit me straight away. We were back in that room where the tunnel had brought us out. And the sounds were echoey, hard, like in a dairy where the floor and walls were covered in tiles. I tried not to think of what was up on the high shelves, floating in those jars of fluid.

"Great dickens!" Miss Stine cried from deep within the room. "You were told to use our special knock!"

"I did." Mr. Walton pushed me forward so I stumbled. "Here's your audience, as requested."

"Bring her in." Then to me, "My experiment on you didn't go as planned, Lizzie. So you'll now observe another procedure. I appreciate you won't see what occurs. But you'll hear what we do and perhaps sense it too."

I felt a surge of panic. "Haven't you seen enough of me? Can't I just go home?"

"If I let you go now, you'll run off with the idea that my work is evil. You'll tell people, who'll tell other people, and my reputation will be ruined."

"I won't tell anyone. I promise."

"I can't risk it, Lizzie. As you're here, and the storm is still raging, I want you to witness what wonders science can achieve. What we couldn't perform on you tonight, we'll try on this poor beast instead. Then you will not fail to understand the potential life-giving properties of electricity."

Before I could object, Miss Stine guided me further into the room. The smell changed to the meaty stench of blood. My stomach turned queasily.

"Put this on," she said, handing me what felt like an apron.

In the end she had to help me because my fingers were shaking and I couldn't tie a knot at the back. Nor could I bear to think what awful things might splash onto my nightgown without it.

"Stand here at the table." Miss Stine placed me on her right side. She directed Mr. Walton and Mr. Cox to stand opposite us.

"Now," she said, "let us begin."

Chapter 24

"ON THE TABLE WE HAVE an animal, killed instantly by a single gunshot wound to the neck," said Miss Stine. Then, with a break in her voice, "I had planned to use rats for my experiments. This beauty, I hoped, would be brought back alive."

"But he escaped again, miss," Mr. Cox said. "He was dangerous. We had to shoot."

She didn't reply.

"He's a fine specimen, though, isn't he?" She sounded almost fond of him: it made me think of how I'd spoken to my geese. "We had two to begin with. We'd hoped to breed from them, but our female died, so we had her preserved. She was a beauty too, you see, and we kept her in a glass case . . . though she didn't fare too well on the journey here."

My face warmed at the memory of Peg clinging to that dead dog. But Miss Stine had already moved on.

"Which," she said, "makes this creature lying before us here the last wolf in England."

I covered my mouth with my hand.

Wolf.

She really did just say *wolf*.

Instinctively I took a step back from the table. Mam had

told us stories—thrilling, glittering stories—of wolves preying on sheep and goats and tiny children in their cribs. And heaven help you if you saw one coming towards you across the snow, all yellow-eyed and slavering. "Oh, Lizzie, they don't live in *England,* not nowadays," she'd laughed, hugging me when I'd gone stiff with terror.

Yet one did live here at Eden Court. Numerous times it had escaped into *our* village, killing *our* livestock. I didn't suppose the locals would believe the truth, not for one minute. The evidence was right in front of me, and I was struggling to believe it myself.

"Come closer to the table, Lizzie," Miss Stine said, pressing her hand into the small of my back.

I took a shaky step forward. The animal smelled of blood and filth. But underneath was just enough of that earthy, woody scent to make me sure it was the same creature I'd heard in our hedge that night. Being this close to it now, I felt a strange mix of fear and awe.

"If this goes to plan, you'll witness something truly incredible," Miss Stine said. "But before you do, I'd like you to touch the wolf, to feel how dead it is."

And suddenly, I didn't know why, but I *wanted* to. I took a step closer. My hand hovered, unsure where to start.

"Begin at the head," said Miss Stine. "The wound is on the underside of its neck. Avoid it if you can—it's rather bloody."

The first things I felt were its ears. They were wet from the rain and surprisingly soft and small. And cold. Then on to the head, which felt as sleek as a house dog's, and a muzzle, now shut, that made my heart skip faster. After the head, the neck and shoulder fur got coarser. My fingers sank into its thickness.

"Is he gray?" I asked.

"Yes," Miss Stine said. "He's a male, caught in the Alps as a juvenile. Shipped over here for study. *Canis lupus:* the gray wolf. In appearance he's dark gray on his upper body and cream-colored on his underside. His eyes are yellow."

I nodded. Moving on, I felt the wolf's flanks, the ribs underneath, and the lean sinew of his long legs and the paws as big as a dancing bear's. The sheer *animalness* took my breath away. I imagined him alive—running, panting, watching with marigold eyes.

And then.

He ended in a sad tail hanging limp off the end of the table. I blinked. I wouldn't cry.

"Very good," murmured Miss Stine beside me.

It didn't *seem* good. By rights, I should have been glad he was dead. Instead, I felt miserable. This was a wild animal. We didn't understand him, and so we were meddling with him when he should have been left in peace, to roam about the mountains with his own kind.

The rain, still driving hard against the window, seemed to echo my bleak thoughts.

"He's dead. We should leave him be," I said.

"Aye," Mr. Cox agreed.

Mr. Walton gave a smug, self-satisfied "hmmm." "Do you hear that, Miss Stine?" he said. "Your audience objects."

"That will change when they see what I'm planning for our dear dead wolf," she replied.

She moved quickly across the room. From behind me came the sounds of jars being opened, of metal scraping metal. My stomach twisted with dread. Moments later, she was back beside me.

"First," she said, "I'll remove the shot from his neck."

I gulped.

"Oh heck." Mr. Cox sounded terrified.

"Mr. Cox, you killed him," Miss Stine said. "I'm merely restoring him to life."

I'd known it was coming. But I still couldn't quite grasp what she was saying.

"Mr. Walton," she said. "Pass me that blade."

A great flash of lightning made everything suddenly white, then blackest black. Bit by bit the black turned to gray, and I saw people-shaped shadows again: one, nearest me, was hunched over the table; the other two opposite held lights aloft. There was no mistaking how those candle flames trembled.

The other details I couldn't see. Didn't want to either. The sounds and smells were enough to make a person faint. I was beginning to wonder if Miss Stine was even human, the way she leant in close, cutting and slicing without hesitation. We could have been witnessing her pulling a tooth, for all the fuss she made.

Yet as the minutes passed, I grew less aware of that bloody smell. The squelching and the snipping and the tug of knife against flesh became noises almost like any other. Miss Stine's actions were neat. Precise. It made me think of Da at work on a length of wood. At last, the shot came out, landing with a ping in a metal pail.

"I'll close the wound now," Miss Stine said, and in moments that was done too. I'd known petticoats take longer to mend.

The lightning came again. One flash, then two more. Just a few beats between and we heard thunder. The air around me seemed to fizz. My hair, crackling, lifted off my shoulders.

I imagined how it must look—mad and stuck out like spun sugar. No one was watching me now, though. Miss Stine, snapping her fingers, barked out orders.

"The wires! Quickly! And the cutthroat razor—is it sharp enough?"

I was aware of people rushing. Of heavy objects being lifted down off shelves and lids being pried open. Amidst the activity, I reached out to touch it again. The wolf lay very still. My fingers found a forepaw, already cool and stiffening. If Miss Stine was right, then the wolf's life force had gone. Without it, he was no more alive than a piece of oak or beech.

"Don't touch him now!" Miss Stine nudged me aside. "You'll ruin his electricity. Stay where you are."

I sensed myself only a short distance from the table. Close enough to still smell the wolf. To hear the frantic rubbing of skin against fur.

"Why are you doing that?" I asked.

"To create static. It helps carry the electrical charge. Mr. Walton"—she clicked her fingers—"the connectors and the wires, please."

As she leant over the table again, I could almost feel those little metal pieces pressed against my skin, as they'd been not an hour earlier.

"You'll get electricity from the pole on the roof?" I asked.

"Yes. If the lightning strikes, it'll travel down through wires we've set up inside the house. The wolf is attached to those wires on his head, paws and chest."

"Just as you did with me in the drawing room."

"Yes. The wires run into that room too." She said it as if we were discussing wallpaper or carpets. But my teeth chattered with fear.

The wires fixed, Miss Stine straightened. She took a deep breath. I hardly dared think what was going to happen next.

First came a hush.

All I heard was the rain. Lightning flickered around the edges of my eyes. My heart was beating very loud, very fast. Next to me, Miss Stine began to count:

"Three . . . two . . . one . . . NOW!"

All at once, white light filled the room. There was a crackling, spitting sound. I felt heat surge through me, almost lifting me off my feet. Then came an almighty roar. It made my ears sing. I tasted metal. And I was sure the earth had split open and we'd fallen inside.

Only then the roar became a grumble, and I realized it was thunder. The crackling eased. Everything went back to gray.

Then silence.

Miss Stine stepped up to the table to inspect the wolf. She seemed to be picking up each of his legs, for as she moved round him, she'd go quiet, then let something fall with a thud.

"Nothing," she said. "No sign of life."

On the opposite side of the table, Mr. Walton gave a huge, relieved sigh. "That poor animal is better off dead," he said.

I looked up in surprise. He was the last person on earth I'd expected to say this.

"Let me take it outside and bury it, miss," pleaded Mr. Cox.

"Good gracious, men! Where's your mettle?" Miss Stine cried. "I'm not giving up after one attempt! Stand back. We'll try again."

She started counting. This time the lightning struck faster. The flash was dazzling. Again I felt heat and heard strange sizzling sounds.

Then the quiet.

Miss Stine inspected the wolf. "We'll keep trying," she said, when it was clear it hadn't worked. "More static, I think."

She started rubbing his fur again. As she worked, I reached out—I couldn't help myself. I felt a paw. A shoulder, warm to the touch. I dug my fingers deeper into the fur.

Miss Stine grabbed my wrist.

"Lizzie! I've told you not to—" Seeing my face, she froze. "What? What is it?"

"Its shoulder twitched. I swear it just moved."

A scrabbling of claws on the tabletop confirmed it.

Mr. Cox said a prayer out loud.

"Oh . . . my . . . goodness," Mr. Walton said in horror. "What on earth have you done?"

There was a grunt. A creaking of the table. The sound of an animal shaking itself. Then came a soft, low growl.

The last wolf in England was alive and stood before us on its feet.

Chapter 25

"STAND BACK! NO ONE TOUCH it!" Miss Stine cried.

Not that I had plans to. I'd felt the size of it when it had lain out dead; it was as big as a pony. And now, as it stood up, swaying like a drunk, its presence seemed to fill the room.

"'Twas better left dead," said Mr. Cox.

"Too late for that." Mr. Walton spoke through gritted teeth. "What do we do with it now?"

"You can't put it in that cage again," I said, remembering how miserable it had sounded. "Can't you . . . I don't know . . . take it back to where you caught it?"

"And release it back into the wild? Don't be ridiculous," Mr. Walton snapped.

"Quiet! All of you! I can't think for your prattling!" cried Miss Stine.

Her voice—shrill, excitable—made the wolf panic. It leapt from the table, dragging wires and knives with it in a whirlwind of legs, tongue, fur. It knocked me into Miss Stine.

"Stay still!" she gasped. "No one move!"

I cowered in fright. What I heard now was the ticking and scrabbling of claws on tiles as the wolf did a frenzied lap of the room. It crashed against the window, the walls. Candles were knocked flying. Bottles smashed to the floor. The air filled with its animal stink.

"It's gone berserk! It needs shooting!" Mr. Cox cried.

Eventually, the wolf slowed and began sniffing the ground.

"I'll fetch my rifle, shall I?" Mr. Cox said shakily.

Miss Stine almost laughed. "After what I've done? Don't you realize what you've just witnessed, Mr. Cox?"

I did.

Part of me felt as stunned and dazed as the wolf itself. Miss Stine had just brought a dead animal back to life, and she'd done it using electricity—lightning—the very thing that had killed Mam and left me blind. I didn't understand the static and the metal and how much was too much, only that somehow she'd made it work. It was an amazing, jaw-dropping thing.

I felt a giddy rush of excitement. What if electricity could bring humans back to life, as it had done the wolf? With Miss Stine's equipment and knowledge, Mam could still be here now. And Peg and Da and Mercy: I'd never have to lose them either, or visit their sad, sorry graves in the churchyard.

It was almost too much to hope for.

No wonder Miss Godwin had been so thrilled. Anyone who'd lost someone dear would wish for this. Yet my excitement quickly grew cold. There were other issues, other problems, and not just the unsettled feeling that had taken hold of me. Miss Stine had done something miraculous, but it left us with a very dangerous animal on our hands. And that smell . . . *that smell* . . .

"Something's burning," I said.

No one heard me: they were too busy bickering. The wolf, snapping and growling, sounded ready to spring.

"Pass me the broom," Mr. Walton said.

"A rifle's the weapon you really want, sir," said Mr. Cox.

"If either of you so much as touches that animal, I'll dismiss you both on the spot!" Miss Stine cried.

"Dismiss us?" Mr. Walton said. "Ha! We'll have to get out of here alive first!"

"Oh, don't be so theatrical!"

"I'm being *practical*!"

Miss Stine breathed deeply. "Then I don't wish to hear your practicality, Mr. Walton. It didn't save your men in the Arctic, did it? I don't believe it will save you now. The wolf is simply frightened. It won't bite."

I wasn't so sure. The wolf was making a strange growling noise in its throat. The burning smell had got stronger too. There wasn't a fire alight in this room. Yet I could detect smoke.

In order to get electricity, the storm had to strike the roof pole; that was what Miss Stine had said. And I knew what happened to things hit by lightning. Something was definitely burning. A roof struck by lightning was the likely place for a fire to start. When I thought who was upstairs, sound asleep in bed, my blood turned cold.

Peg.

"Fire!" I said, shaky at first, then in a proper panic. "FIRE! There's a FIRE!"

The door was to my right, I recalled. Stumbling towards it, I bashed against boxes and chairs.

"Stand still! Don't run!" Miss Stine yelled.

Whether she meant me or not, I didn't know. Didn't care.

Then came a scream.

"Arrrgh!" Mr. Walton cried. "Get it off me! I beg you!"

There was a frenzy of claws. Snarling. Snapping. Something sounding horribly wet. Then came a rip, a tearing noise like a rabbit being skinned. And gurgling and gasping that was definitely human.

I blocked out the rest: it was too awful to contemplate. All that mattered was reaching Peg.

Out in the passage, the smoke was already thickening. I couldn't remember the way back to the main part of the house—was it left or right? I went left. The passage ended abruptly in a wall. Cussing myself, I turned and rushed back the way I'd just come. With each stride the smoke got stronger. My throat grew tight and hot. Then, underfoot, the floor changed from flagstones to marble and I knew I'd reached the main hall.

There were people everywhere, shouting and sloshing water and running from room to room. There wasn't a second to lose. Then someone shouted, "Get that girl out of here! It's not safe! Now the attic's alight, the rest of the house won't be far behind."

I'd been spotted.

Footsteps rushed towards me, then faltered. "But I've to fill these water buckets!"

"Do it, then! Quickly!"

In the panic, I was forgotten.

Finding the nearest door, I ducked behind it before anyone could lay hands on me and haul me outside. I pulled the door shut. Now I stood in some sort of dark cupboard, and I didn't know what to do next. The smoke was already making me cough, and I still had to reach Peg.

As I stood fidgeting, my toe hit something unexpectedly hard. It was, I realized, a step. There were more, going up and up. My heart leapt. This wasn't a cupboard. It was a whole flight of stairs, probably the ones used by servants to carry laundry and bedpans so no one important ever saw. Seizing the handrail, I charged upwards.

The stairs didn't stop at a landing. They twisted round and round for what felt like miles. The smoke got thicker. Hotter. Each breath hurt like knives. At the top of the stairs the heat was so fierce it had used up all the air. Above my head, I heard strange hissing sounds. I smelled smoke, wood, burning hair. Bright patterns danced before my eyes. And then came another whoosh of heat.

Peg was in here somewhere. I had to get to her. But I couldn't remember which room was ours. Mam would've known. She'd have been brave enough to keep going too, and not stand around dithering.

"Think, Lizzie, think," I said out loud. Immediately I started coughing. My only hope was to do what I'd done before and feel along the wall.

I moved down the passage, my free hand covering my mouth. Above me, the hissing sound grew louder. The smoke was so thick I could taste it. Sweat stuck my hair to my face and neck.

Suddenly I tripped, lurching forward into space and falling hard on my knees. But when I stood up again, I laughed out loud. That stupid single step had caught me out last time. It meant I was right outside our room.

The bedroom door was already open.

"Peg?" I cried. "Are you there? Wake up! I've come to get you!"

Tripping over those same blasted chairs, I somehow found my way to the bed. The sheets were thrown back. The bed was empty. My legs sagged with relief. But there wasn't time to even gather my wits. Right above me, the ceiling groaned.

Dust fell in my face. In my mouth. Gasping, I found the door again, the single step in the passageway. Then I had to stop and throw up.

At the top of the staircase, I hesitated. My head felt as if it were lifting off my shoulders. But it didn't matter. Nothing mattered. Peg had got out. She was safe. All was going to be fine. Before my eyes everything seemed to sparkle. Then the walls closed in around me.

Chapter 26

I CAME TO LYING ON my back. I was outside on wet grass, and it was still raining. For a moment I simply lay there, letting the wetness seep into my skin. I'd been sick again, and the smell of that and the smoke made my head hurt. When I did open my eyes, I was aware of something very light and bright blazing through the trees.

"You're all right. We got you out just in time," said a familiar-sounding person, pushing a cup of water into my hand. It was Ruth the maid. "Don't think they're going to save the house, though."

I sat up shakily. "Is my sister here? Did she get out?"

"Shh, easy now," she said. "Your sister got out, yes."

"Oh, thank goodness!" The relief set me coughing again.

"Here, sip some of this water." She took the cup and raised it to my mouth. "Miss Stine and Mr. Walton weren't with you, were they? No one can find them anywhere. I can't bear to think what's happened."

I couldn't bear to either. Though I'd never forget what it felt like to touch a wolf, to sink my fingers into its fur and feel twitching muscle beneath. Nor would I forget the sound of Mr. Walton's screams. Both would haunt me forever.

I took another sip of water. It was best just to think about finding Peg.

"Where is my sister, then?" I asked, supposing she was out here on the grass somewhere.

"She's gone, went quite a while ago," said Ruth.

"Gone? Back to the village?"

She didn't answer.

"What's happened?" I said. "Where's Peg?"

"She left with the guests a couple of hours back," said Ruth in a nervous rush. "Took off in a right hurry, they did, and I know I shouldn't say this for worrying you, but your sister didn't seem as if she wanted to go. It was just after they got the news that Miss Godwin's father had come looking for her. Asked Mr. Cox's son to drive them all the way to the coast so they could catch an early boat to France and then on to Switzerland. I heard them say they were taking Peg with them...."

"To the Villa Diodati," I murmured. Despite everything, that faraway-sounding name had stuck in my head.

With it came a terrifying thought.

Of Peg strapped to a chair just like I'd been, wires fixed to her head. Of Miss Godwin almost delirious with the hope Miss Stine had given her.

Was *that* why they'd taken her?

Did they want Miss Stine's experiment to work so much that they were willing to practice it themselves on Peg? They'd been happy enough to watch Miss Stine work on me, and desperate enough to take a child against her wishes.

And now I was too late to save her.

Or was I? Ruth was saying something about muddy roads. "They'll be lucky if they make that early boat after all this rain."

I scrambled to my feet. If I reached the coast by daybreak, I just might be able to get to Peg before she and Miss Godwin's party set sail for the Continent.

Yet by the time I arrived in Sweepfield, so too had news of the fire. The streets were as busy as day and full of talk.

"The whole of Eden Court is alight, with little chance of saving it," someone said.

"Aye, 'tis terrible!" said someone else. "All that furniture and silver. 'Tis worth more than this village put together."

"I heard they can't find that Walton chap, the scientist."

No one mentioned Miss Stine. But then, why would they? They probably didn't know she existed.

"Pardon me, but my sister's missing," I interrupted. "I need to go after her. Can any of you help me reach the coast?"

I didn't think they'd heard me. So I tried again. "Can anyone take me to the coast, please? I beg of you."

"We know your sister's missing, Lizzie Appleby, and that your da's gone off to fetch her back," one of the speakers said. "Now go on home and leave it to him. Everyone here's busy with the fire tonight."

I began to panic. "But she got snatched by those people at Eden Court, and now they've gone off in a carriage to catch a boat!"

"Listen to her. She's not right in the head, she in't," another person said, meaning me. "And fancy being outside in a filthy nightgown."

Coming as I had from the fire, I'd forgotten what a state I must look. I wrapped my arms around myself to try to hide the worst of it. I'd grown cold too. The rain had stopped, but the night air was very cool.

"You must help me, please!" I cried.

"Go home, miss," the first voice said again. It was obvious these people weren't going to offer any assistance.

I went further on, past the village green and the church, and the turning for Mill Lane. Folks stood in doorways gossiping. There were sounds of horses being saddled and buckets being gathered up. Plenty of help was on offer for Eden Court, so it seemed.

"Is anyone traveling to the coast?" I asked, stopping everyone I could. "I need to follow our Peg. She was taken in a carriage from Eden Court earlier tonight."

"Planned that well, then, didn't she, to get out just before the fire," said a woman from her doorstep.

I stared in the direction of her voice. "She isn't responsible, if that's what you mean."

"No, course she in't. Like she weren't responsible for those animals going missing neither."

"But she isn't! She's done nothing wrong!"

"Aye, so you've said," the woman said, and shut her door on me.

I stood there reeling. And though I tried very hard not to cry or to scream, I was on the verge of doing both.

So this was what it had come to. Peg was being blamed—we as a *family* were being blamed. From now on, every time bad luck befell Sweepfield it would be our doing. Never mind fate or the stars or pure and simple bad weather. It was all down to those Applebys, whose mother always did have too much to say for herself and got what she deserved in the end.

"Lizzie? What are you doing down there?"

I looked up. "Mercy? Is that you?"

"Of course it's me, you idiot!"

Without realizing it, I'd walked as far as the bakery. Some feet above my head, Mercy leant out her bedchamber window. I was so glad that tears rolled down my cheeks.

"What the heck's happened to you?" she asked with a gasp. "You look dreadful!"

"Never mind that now," I said. "I need your help. Some people have snatched Peg and I have to go after her."

"I'll come with you," Mercy said. The window shut as she disappeared inside.

"No, Mercy! Wait!" I cried.

The window opened again. "What is it?"

"This is proper serious. I need to get to the coast by morning."

"The *coast*? Blimey, Lizzie, what's going on?"

I didn't know where to start, so I kept it simple.

"Peg's been taken by a Mr. Shelley and a Miss Godwin who were staying at Eden Court. They're catching a boat across the Channel first thing. If I'm to get Peg back, then I need to leave Sweepfield tonight."

"So I can't come with you?"

Dear Mercy.

It was a struggle not to accept her offer. Her eyes would be a great help, her company even more so. Yet this was a grim, ugly business. It didn't seem right to drag her into it, especially when she had responsibilities of her own.

"Your mam needs you here in the shop," I said. "And it'll be easier to hitch a ride if there's just one of us. Fingers crossed I'll be back in a day or two."

There was the chance I would not be, though, not if I didn't make the boat. I'd go all the way to Switzerland if I had to. I wouldn't come back without Peg. I think Mercy guessed as much.

"All right," she said after a long pause. "Wait there a minute." A moment of quiet, then she was back at the window. "Here, put these on."

Something soft fell beside me on the cobbles. Then a heavier *thud—thud*. Feeling around, I found a clean dress, a shawl that smelled of baking and Mercy's old clogs.

"Thank you." I dragged the clothes on quickly and felt better for it. "If my da comes back before me, tell him where I've gone."

"I will. Good luck, Lizzie. Your mam would be proud of you."

I smiled. "Thank you." Then, out of nowhere, I remembered Isaac. "Have you seen Isaac Blake today?"

"Huh! Why'd I want to see him?" she said, suddenly sulky.

"Have you *seen* him?" I repeated.

"He came to the shop this morning when we were really busy. Kept coming back and all, so Mam told him to clear off. He's been here tonight too, chucking stones at my window. Said he needed to talk to me urgently. I thought you were him again, to be honest."

It was a relief to hear that Isaac was back in the village and not stuck somewhere inside that burning house. I'd hoped he'd come to Mercy to raise the alarm, or at least tell her about me disappearing from the barn where he'd left me. And as it sounded as if he'd tried, he might still be willing to help.

"Don't think too badly of him, Mercy," I said. "He's a decent sort, really."

"What d'you mean? I thought you hated him?"

"I've seen a better side to him today. And he's still proper daft about you, you know."

After saying my goodbyes to Mercy, I hurried down the street. I just hoped I could find my way to Isaac's farm. Not twenty yards further on, I came across two men having a heated debate.

"Not likely! Not on these roads. It's a good thirty miles to the coast from here. You'll never make it by morning!"

"I *have* to make it, sir. Otherwise my daughter's ship will have sailed and my mission to find her will have been in vain."

This second speaker didn't sound local. From what he was saying, it soon became clear who he was.

"Then you'd do better keeping a closer eye on her in the first place, wouldn't you? Daughters are going missing left, right and flipping center round here these days."

"So you won't help me, then?"

"How can I? You'll need a carthorse to get through this mud."

"And who might have one of those around here?"

I knew the answer; I was seeking the same thing myself.

Clearing my throat, I tapped what I hoped was the right man's arm.

"If you're Mr. Godwin and your daughter is called Mary, then I reckon I can be of assistance to you."

And Mr. Godwin, with his eyes that worked, would definitely be of help to me.

Chapter 27

AS WE TRUDGED THROUGH THE mud towards Dipcott, Mr. Godwin talked amiably enough of London and his shop that sold books. Though I half listened, I kept thinking of our Peg and why his daughter had taken her. In the end I had to ask.

"I've no idea," he said. "It's most baffling. Though my daughter is rather prone to impulsive actions—her dear departed mother was too. Poor Mary, she lost her own child, a baby girl, not so long ago. It did affect her deeply. But really, taking another child is no sort of solution. How awful this must be for your family."

His answer did little to ease my fears.

The one person I thought might help us was Isaac Blake. Living as he did outside the village, he hadn't heard about the fire at Eden Court or the commotion surrounding it. It also meant he was pretty hard to wake up.

"Are you certain this is the right window?" Mr. Godwin asked, when he'd thrown countless stones at the glass.

"I have it on good authority from Mercy Matthews that it is."

Just to be certain, I asked him to throw one last stone really hard. Within seconds, the window swung open.

"What the flying blazes is going on?" Isaac cried. Then, sounding more confused, "Lizzie. What the ... I mean ... crikey ... you're here!"

"It is me, yes. Now I need ..."

Isaac kept talking. "What happened to you this morning? I tried to come back for you, but Jeffers carted me off the premises. And when I got back to the village I went straight to tell Mercy, but she wouldn't listen."

So my hunch was right: he *had* tried to raise the alarm.

"Isaac, we need your help. Desperately, as it happens."

"We?"

Stepping forward from the shadows, Mr. Godwin introduced himself and explained about his daughter.

"There's been a fire at Eden Court," I added. "The place is in ruins."

Typically, Isaac's first thought was of pigs. "So even if they hadn't thrown me out and told me never to come back, they'd still not be wanting half a porker tomorrow?"

"I reckon not." If the wolf survived the fire, he doubtless wouldn't escape Mr. Cox's gun. I was dying to tell Isaac all I'd discovered, but it'd have to wait. "So can you help us? We need to reach the coast by morning."

Isaac didn't miss a beat.

"At your service," he said.

He was quick about it too, harnessing his carthorse and backing him into the shafts of a cart, all within a matter of minutes. Once we'd climbed on board, Isaac shook the reins. The cart groaned; the wheels spun; then, with a massive lurch, we were off.

The first few miles were slow going. Cartwheels and hooves sprayed mud in all directions. The slithering, swaying motion made me feel awful queasy, or maybe it was still the effects of the fire. Yet once we reached the main road, I sat up eagerly in my seat, for I knew this road well. It was the old ridgeway that ran right along the tops of the hills. The road was straight, and mostly smooth, dry chalk; on either side of it, the moors fell away. On a clear night up here the stars shone bright as lamps. Mam said it was a special, ancient place; I could almost feel it tingling against my skin.

For many more miles, we sat squashed together on the hard little bench seat. The ground grew steadily more rutted and rock-strewn, so eventually the smooth ridgeway was but a distant dream. Every jolt, every jar of the road, went through my backside, all the way up to my teeth. My head throbbed. My shoulders ached. I began to dream of walking those last few miles—anything to stop the feeling that my bones were like dice in a cup.

Suddenly the road dipped sharply. The horse panicked, its back hooves slipping beneath it. Isaac talked gently until it shook its head, ready to move on. We passed under the darkness of trees, then came out in a bumpy lane. By now the smell had changed from mud to salt, and the birdsong on the breeze was that of gulls. I hugged my knees to my chest in an effort to stay warm. Mr. Godwin, I noticed, had gone very quiet.

The road took us to a tollgate; then the mud became cobbles as we entered the town. The sun was up and bright, and the streets sounded unnaturally busy.

"Hurry!" I cried. "Oh, do hurry!"

We sped along at a ragged trot. I could only imagine how mud-splattered and windswept we looked, but all that mattered was reaching the boat. We had no time to lose.

"Is it in dock? Can you see anything?" I asked, rising up in my seat.

"Only your knees. Sit down!" Isaac said.

As we took a left turn, the road got even busier. Everyone seemed to be traveling in the opposite direction from us.

"This don't look good," Isaac said.

"Keep going, young man," Mr. Godwin replied. "We won't know if it's sailed until we get there."

I sat on my hands to stop them from fidgeting. The boat couldn't have gone yet: it was only just daybreak. But a horrible dragging feeling began pulling at my insides. A right turn and the smell of fishing nets grew stronger, until finally Isaac heaved on the reins. The cart slowed, then stopped.

"Here we are," he said. "This is as close as I can get to the harbor side."

All around us drivers shouted and clicked tongues at their horses. Carriages turned and moved on. There were people on foot. Crowds of them. Laughing, talking, selling things fresh from the sea, all in accents thicker than ours at home.

"You'd best climb down. The proper harbor is just around the corner. You can't see nothing from here," Isaac said, sensing my hesitation. "I'll find a place to park up and wait for you."

I nodded. Then I patted Isaac's arm.

"You're a good sort, Isaac Blake," I heard myself saying. "I might've been wrong about you and Mercy. Go and have another word with her when you get back."

He gave an embarrassed cough. "Oh. Right. Well." I pictured his ears going red.

The cart creaked as Mr. Godwin stepped down. I followed, landing heavily on the cobbles so my feet stung. He took my elbow and together we made our way through the crowds to the water's edge. Every now and then, he stopped people to ask if they'd seen Miss Godwin.

"We're looking for a young woman, eighteen years of age. Small in stature, long, reddish-gold hair. She's with another young woman of similar age, and a tall, rather thin man."

"And a girl in a green frock," I added. "With curly white-blond hair."

No one had seen them.

When we reached the harbor side, it sounded quiet. Too quiet.

"Can you see a sailing ship? Is it here? Can we reach it?" I said in a rush.

Mr. Godwin didn't speak for a very long moment.

"There is a sailing ship, yes." His voice cracked with feeling. "By my reckoning it's about half a mile off shore."

My heart sank to the cobbles. We were too late.

"There we are, then. We did try." Mr. Godwin sniffed and blew his nose. "Maybe they'll return someday."

"But, sir, they've gone to Switzerland, not the moon," I said.

"My dear, I am too old to go chasing across Europe. So indeed, it might as well be the moon to me. Good day to you." And he went off in search of a coach to take him back to London.

I stared after him in amazement. Was that it, then? Was he giving up? I only hoped our da had more staying power: I knew I did.

For once, though, I didn't think of what Mam would've done. I didn't listen for her voice inside my head. This time, I trusted my own judgment. I'd get Peg even if it did mean going to France, then Switzerland and on to the Villa Diodati.

There was bound to be another boat tomorrow.

3

Ideas Set Free

VILLA DIODATI, LAKE GENEVA

JUNE 1816

Chapter 28

LIZZIE SPOKE UNTIL MORNING. THEN, as light seeped in under the shutters, her head finally slumped forward. Felix grew alarmed: *She isn't . . . is she?* The rise and fall of her chest told him no, she wasn't dead. She'd simply fallen asleep.

Relieved, he got to his feet, stretching his legs, which had grown stiff from too much sitting in expensive chairs.

"I must go to bed," said Mary, rubbing her eyes. "Fetch me when she wakes, will you?"

"I expect she'll come to you first," Felix replied. "She's very set on getting her sister back."

Mary frowned. "So you believe her? You think the child we brought with us from Eden Court *is* her sister?"

Looking down at the sleeping girl, Felix knew now who she reminded him of. Her hair was dark blond, not white. Straight, not curled. Yet she resembled that face he'd seen yesterday at the Shelleys' window. She must truly love her little sister to come all this way from England, blind *and* on her own.

"Lizzie's ever so brave," Felix said.

Mary stood up and smoothed her dress. "She tells a good story, I'll grant her that."

Felix stared at Mary.

"She hasn't come just to tell a story," he said. "What she's told us seems to be the truth."

"Oh," Mary faltered. "Oh, I see. . . . Dear me . . . So you *do* believe what she said?"

"I think so, yes. It's your friend you should be more concerned about. This Miss Stine isn't all she seems."

Mary sank heavily into her chair again. She looked pale and suddenly lost.

"You're right," she said, head in her hands. "Though it pains me to admit it, Lizzie's account of what happened at Eden Court is a fair one. We were part of something awful that night; we encouraged it."

When Mary glanced up, her face was full of despair. "Oh, Felix. I believe I've made the most terrible mistake."

In less than an hour, Lizzie awoke.

"My sister! Is she here? Is she safe?" She tried to get up, only to fall back onto the chaise longue.

"Hush, you're still weak," Mary said. "In a few days, when you're stronger, we'll take you to her."

Felix, though, didn't think it should wait. And he was getting rather used to speaking his mind.

"Mary, your house is but a short walk away," he said. "It's best for everyone if we do it today."

Now it was Mary who looked scared—and terribly tired. He felt it too—that grittiness in his eyes and the throb in his head. In the end, it was agreed they'd have breakfast first.

When they came to leave, they found the front door was bolted.

"Who is this person following you, Lizzie?" Felix asked, recalling why he'd locked the door last night.

"Not following *me*, exactly. She caught the same boat across the Channel, but she probably had a smart cabin, whereas I slept in the hold. I didn't even know she was on board till we docked in France."

Felix caught Mary's eye. The look they shared said *Miss Stine*.

"So you think she's coming here?" he asked, nervous.

"I know it. I heard her on the quayside, bartering for a ride to Switzerland. I'd recognize that voice anywhere, honest I would."

"Did she mention Diodati?" Mary asked.

"She mentioned *you*, miss. It seems she's carrying some sort of heavy luggage, something she wants you to see. But none of the carters would take it. They sounded scared, to be frank, and made excuses about their carts being too small, their horses too old. I had to reach Peg before she got here. I don't trust her, miss. Not an inch."

"We'd better hurry, then," Felix said. "Mary's villa isn't far."

Outside, the storm was over, leaving the sky a pale, washed-out blue. The ground was soaked, the trees and bushes heavy with rainwater. By the time they'd gone through the apple orchard to the Shelleys' villa, Felix's stockinged legs were drenched.

As was usual at this time of day, the windows were still shuttered, even the little one where yesterday Felix had seen the child's face. Mary guided them inside through the front door.

"It'll be best not to wake Percy or Claire," she explained. "We don't want a scene."

201

They tiptoed through the silent house and up uneven stairs that made Lizzie stumble. Felix, gripping her arm as best he could, noticed how she trembled. Inside the attic bedroom, it was just light enough for him to see a narrow bed and a shape lying still beneath the covers.

"Clara, dear," Mary said gently, going to the bed and sitting on its edge. "There's someone here to see you."

The sleeping person didn't move.

"Clara?" Lizzie frowned.

Felix took a sharp breath: Clara was the name of Mary's baby who'd died. At last, he began to understand why she might've done this, why she'd taken another child and tried to make it her own. She couldn't save her own daughter, yet she could perhaps offer Lizzie's troubled little sister a better life. It still seemed a strange, misguided thing to do, but perhaps it had been done in good heart.

Breaking free of Felix, Lizzie rushed towards Mary's voice. "Peg! Oh, Peg!"

The shape under the covers sat up so fast it made Felix jump.

"Lizzie? Is that you? Is Da here?"

A girl emerged from under the covers. It was hard to see her properly, for though Mary had opened the shutters by now, the bed was a tangle of arms and hair and weeping.

"Thank goodness I found you," Lizzie sobbed. "We'll send word to Da that you're safe. He'll be so, so relieved. Oh, Peg."

Watching silently, Felix felt his throat grow thick. He hoped Mary was watching too, for, hard though this was for her, there was no doubting that these two girls were sisters. Eventually, they moved apart—Lizzie, her eyes red from crying, and Peg, whose face stretched into a grin as she noticed Felix.

"I saw you yesterday when I looked out my window, didn't I? Who are you?" she asked.

"He's—"

"That's—"

"I'm Felix," he said, cutting across Mary and Lizzie. He stepped forwards, hand outstretched. "Very pleased to meet you, Peg."

She couldn't take her eyes off his face. He guessed she'd never met a boy with dark skin before. Seizing his hand, she shook it so hard their arms swung, and it made them both laugh.

Mary stood a little apart from them at the window. It was the old Mary again: composed, quiet. But underneath it, Felix was sure her heart was breaking. He knew a little of how that felt, hoping for a future with someone only to lose them.

Letting go of Peg, he joined her in looking up at the sky.

"The comet's still up there," he observed. Today it looked even smaller and fainter.

"And the cause of much bad fortune, so people say," Lizzie said from where she sat on the bed.

Felix narrowed his eyes at the sky. His mother came to mind. Back when their boat set sail for Europe she'd stood on deck and said even the stars were in their favor.

"Look!" she'd cried, pointing up at the night sky. "Look!" Yet he'd seen nothing but darkness.

Today the sky was bright. The sun was coming up over the mountains; it promised to be a better day, not just for Lizzie, who had found her sister, but for him too. These past few hours he'd done well to keep his head. Mary had listened to him, relied on him. He'd proved himself to be more than just a houseboy. If he could go to London with Lord Byron, then perhaps he wouldn't be stared at for the color of his skin. People would value him for who he really was and life might be very good indeed.

Mary, meanwhile, remained solemn.

"A comet won't decide your fortune, Lizzie," she said. "How can it? It's just rock and ice, so the scientists say."

Lizzie looked suddenly thoughtful. "Before she died, my mam laughed about comets bringing bad luck. Then all these dreadful things happened to us and I felt sure the comet was to blame. But maybe my mam was right after all."

"It looks like a star," Felix said.

"A star with a tail," Peg added, joining them at the window.

Mary smiled weakly. "It's not a star either. Though better a star than all that mumbo-jumbo superstition people seem to believe."

"Maybe," Lizzie said, "it's a strange sort of star. Not a normal-looking one but still something beautiful."

Felix nodded. In a room of rather unusual people who, each in their own way, had beauty, he rather liked the sound of that.

"It won't dictate your future, however," Mary commented. "That's something only you can do."

She was right, Felix thought. The future was his to choose. He didn't have to be a boy branded with the letter *S*. He was free—and capable. It was as if he'd got permission to be his very best self, instead of someone who simply met the needs of others.

From outside came the sound of an approaching horse. On the road that wound its way around the lake, a cart emerged from behind the trees. It pulled up outside Diodati. Down from it jumped a woman in a cloak, who set off through the orchard towards the Shelleys' house.

Towards them.

"Go!" Mary cried, herding them out of the bedchamber. "It's better that Miss Stine doesn't see you."

Lizzie nodded, a look of absolute fear in her face.

"Don't panic. You're safe," Felix reassured her. "She can't hurt you anymore."

Yet having heard Lizzie's tale, he knew what this Miss Stine was capable of—experimenting on people and animals, stealing children away in the night. He didn't exactly want to meet her either. Better that Mary dealt with it now.

They made it as far as the top of the staircase before Miss Stine started hammering on the front door. Within moments, the entire household was awake.

"What's happening? Is there an emergency?" Mr. Shelley cried, appearing in his nightshirt.

Miss Clairmont rushed after him. "Is it Byron? Has he come calling for me?"

Pushing past Felix, Mary hurried down the stairs. "Percy, Claire, go back to bed. I'll handle this."

They went, grumbling sleepily. Mary beckoned Felix. "If you're quick you can sneak out of the—"

The banging at the door became frantic.

"Mary? I must speak to you!" Miss Stine's cries could clearly be heard. "Everything's gone wrong!"

Frustrated, Mary threw up her hands, before disappearing down the hallway to answer the door.

Felix glanced at Lizzie.

"You ready?" he whispered.

She nodded. Peg looked bewildered, and suddenly very young.

"Keep hold of your big sister's hand," he said to her.

They inched down the stairs. One particular step creaked like an old ship. Felix held his breath as they passed it.

"Which way now?" he asked, once they reached the bottom.

"There's a back door," Peg said.

"Come along, then," said Lizzie.

Peg didn't move. "We can't. It's by the kitchens, which are . . ."

". . . down the hall, past the front door," finished Felix, realizing their problem.

"Oh." Lizzie's hand tightened around Peg's. "Then what do we do? We can't just stand here."

"Hush!" Felix hissed. "Don't fret. We'll have to find somewhere to hide."

He looked around. The hallway was long and narrow, with lots of doors leading off he didn't know where. There was no obvious hiding place. From down the hall came the *click-clack* of footsteps. There were voices too, quick and urgent.

"Oh heck!" Peg whispered. "They're coming!"

Chapter 29

FELIX GRABBED THE NEAREST DOOR and pushed it open. Inside was a sort of parlor. There were books everywhere—on shelves, tables, chairs.

"This'll do," he said, beckoning to the girls.

The door had only just swung shut behind them when, out in the hallway, two sets of footsteps stopped.

"We'll talk in the library," Mary said.

They were coming in.

Felix took Lizzie's arm. "Quick! Duck down!"

They crouched behind a bookcase as the library door opened. Felix tried to quieten his breathing. He watched as Mary led someone into the room, shutting the door behind them. The woman was small like Mary, with yellow hair peeping out from under a bonnet.

So this was Miss Stine.

She didn't look like a scientist. But then, he supposed, he didn't know what one *did* look like. More worryingly, he and Lizzie and Peg weren't well hidden. If Miss Stine glanced round, she'd see the tops of three heads. Lizzie clearly sensed this; she'd put her hand over Peg's mouth.

Miss Stine wasn't shown to a seat. She stood, twisting her

hands. "I come to you in deep despair, Mary. The night you left there was a fire at Eden Court. It destroyed all my work, all my findings. The house couldn't be saved—everything perished."

Mary eyed her coldly. "Yes, I did hear as much."

"You read of it in the papers?"

"No, I *heard* of it, Francesca, from someone who was there."

Miss Stine's finger-twisting stopped. Her hands, gripped together, turned white at the knuckles. "So the girl survived the fire after all. That night someone saw her in the hallway trying to go upstairs, so I assumed she'd not survived."

"Bet she wishes I *was* dead," Lizzie muttered under her breath.

"She came all this way for her sister," Mary said. "And now that I've heard the truth of what went on that night at Eden Court, I'm very sorry I ever showed an interest in your work."

"Look here!" Miss Stine's voice suddenly rose. "You mustn't believe the girl. I tried to convince her that my ideas could work. I showed her *everything,* Mary. So if that little traitor has now come to you spreading evil lies about my experiments, as I feared she would, I swear I'll make her sorry—and that brat sister of hers!"

Beside him, Felix sensed Lizzie stiffen. She held Peg tight to her chest.

"I suggest you drop that tone," Mary said icily.

But Miss Stine kept on. "Where are the girls? Let me see them at once!"

She'd started pacing the room too, which made Felix very nervous. Though they'd shrunk down further behind the book-case, she'd only have to peer behind it to see them.

"Enough, Francesca!" Mary cried. Taking hold of Miss

Stine's arms at the elbows, she looked deep into the scientist's face. "You must stop. You've caused enough trouble already."

The two women stared hard at each other. Then the fight went out of Miss Stine and she dipped her head. "I have nothing left."

Lizzie, still holding Peg, made a little "hmm" sound of disgust. Felix hoped Mary wasn't taken in by it either.

He needn't have worried.

"And you've come to me for *pity?*" Mary said, letting go of her and taking a step back.

Miss Stine looked shocked. "Well, I hoped you might help me get back on course. I have *nothing:* I mean it, Mary. I can't stop my research now, not when it's—"

"All your life you've had too much of everything," Mary interrupted. "Too much ambition, too many ideas, even too much money."

"It was my father's money and his father's money," Miss Stine said. "I hardly think—"

"Money got from sugar plantations. From other people's misery," Mary said grimly. "You told me once how your grandfather insisted on branding all his slaves with the letter *S,* even the babies. I've never forgotten it."

Felix's hand went to his arm. Was *this* what the S shape of his scar meant—*S* for *Stine?*

He felt dazed.

He didn't know whether it was some awful coincidence or a reminder that there were others, many others, with scars like his. There was so much he wanted to feel. So much he wanted to say. And yet, as he stared at Miss Stine, all he saw was a rather small, badly dressed woman. She had no power over anyone in the room. And she certainly didn't own him.

"You say you have nothing?" Mary asked. "I suppose you've come to us for money, as my father often does."

"Well, yes, I'm afraid I have. All my family's money has gone in debts and so forth. I hoped maybe Percy could help me with a loan from his inheritance."

Mary shook her head very firmly. "No, Francesca. That won't be possible. You see, we've lost something too. The girl you so kindly *arranged* for us to adopt isn't an orphan after all. She has a family who love her and who've come to claim her."

Miss Stine faltered.

The room went quiet. Miss Stine had started twisting her hands again. Yet it was Mary now whom Felix couldn't take his eyes off. She looked ready to commit murder.

"Why did you let me take the girl?" she asked. "Why did you set it all up?"

"To ease your grief," Miss Stine said, her voice trembling. "I couldn't bring your daughter back to life—not yet, anyway; my work isn't that advanced—and it pained me to see you still suffering from Clara's death."

So this daughter of slave owners had *feelings*? Felix was keen to hear what they were.

"I wanted to *do* something for you, Mary," Miss Stine said. "As your friend."

It made Felix think suddenly of Dr. Polidori and his sprained ankle. People had a habit of doing odd things to impress Miss Godwin and Mr. Shelley. This, though, was quite something else.

"And you just *happened* to have a random child at your disposal?" Mary said.

"Please, there was a mistake. Mr. Walton brought me the wrong girl. It was Lizzie Appleby I wanted to study, not her little sister. But when I heard her story—she said she had no mother and that the villagers spoke ill of her—I thought you could give her a new beginning."

"So you lied? You planned all this yourself?"

"I . . . well . . ."

"Good grief, Francesca!" Mary spat. "You're not just clever—you're twisted!"

"And now I'm ruined." Miss Stine's shoulders visibly sagged. "All I have left to show for a lifetime of work is a wolf."

Felix glanced sideways at Lizzie. The color had drained from her cheeks.

"Not so long ago, I believed in your work, Francesca. But I've seen the damage it can do. What you propose is not the answer to people's grief. I'm not sure there really *is* an answer to that." Mary composed herself again. "So I'm afraid I can't help you anymore. As for this wolf business, yes, I've heard about it, but I'm not sure I believe it. Besides, you can't possibly have brought him all this way."

"But there is a wolf! He was shot dead and I brought him back to life!" Miss Stine cried, gesturing towards the door. "He's outside in a crate!"

"Whatever for?"

"As proof that my work should go on. I hoped you of all people would see him and realize what, with time, can be achieved. Forget about what you've heard and listen to me. I have great plans. Great ambitions. The wolf in question came from the Alps originally. I have notions of capturing another from the same pack and giving it a mate."

Mary folded her arms across her chest. "Capturing a wolf? Really, Francesca, this is too much."

"It needs a companion again. Originally it had one but she

died, and being a lone wolf has made it very savage. Do you know it killed my assistant back in England?"

"So Mr. Walton *is* dead," whispered Lizzie. She looked horrified.

Mary didn't speak. Her silence said it all.

"You won't help me?" Miss Stine asked.

Mary shook her head.

"Very well. I'll have to find someone to shoot the wretched creature, won't I?"

"If there really is a wolf, then yes, I suppose you will," Mary replied. "And let me warn you, if you take one step towards the Appleby girls again, I promise I'll see you're sent to Newgate Gaol or somewhere equally awful. Am I understood?"

Wearily, Miss Stine straightened her shoulders. "Yes, Mary, you are."

There didn't seem much left to say. Mary, her manner cold and brittle, showed Miss Stine out of the library. Their footsteps retreated down the hall.

"Mary's right. It's that Francesca Stine who needs putting in a cage," said Lizzie. "I've a good mind to go after her."

Felix stopped her.

"Leave it. It's finished," he said. There were bad people he'd have liked to cut a strip off too. But it didn't make things better; it just made you feel a different sort of awful. "You've got Peg back safely. So try thinking good thoughts, like going home and being with your father again."

Lizzie hugged Peg tighter. "No more of your silly lies, Peg Appleby. You're going home to a family who *loves* you, d'you hear me?"

Peg, looking slightly stunned, nodded.

His feet numb from sitting, Felix stood up. "We should leave."

This time they found the back door easily enough. They startled a kitchen maid who was busy making breakfast, and emerged, blinking, into the sunshine of what was now a rather warm day. Felix found himself thinking of London again—the sun shining on the river, the vast white buildings that he imagined might look like iced cakes.

"How will you both get home?" he asked Lizzie.

"Same way as I came, I suppose."

"Do you have money?" Looking at her shabby dress and worn feet, he guessed she didn't. "Because I've a little bit saved. If you hitch a ride back to France, it might pay your passage across the Channel."

"You've been too kind already. We can't take your money," Lizzie said.

"Yes we can," Peg said. "At least, we could borrow it."

But Lizzie was adamant. "No, we can't. We'll write to Da that we're safe, and we'll find work and earn our way home."

"Then let me ask Frau Moritz if she has need of you," Felix said, for the idea of them both staying on at Diodati a little longer seemed a very fine plan indeed. He suspected Lizzie agreed, for she slipped her arm through his as they walked.

"Felix, you know what you asked back there about good thoughts?" she said.

"Yes."

"Before we go home to England, there's something I want to do here in Switzerland. It's a good thing, and who knows, it might bring peace to us all." Lizzie gave a nervous smile. "It's going to be a bit dangerous, and it'll have to be a secret from everyone else. I'll need both your help. And Peg, it involves an animal, so you're going to absolutely *adore* it."

*   *   *

Back at Diodati, Frau Moritz eyed Lizzie and Peg up and down as if they were pigs ready for market.

"Well, they're both wanting flesh," she observed. Yet like Felix, she was impressed by how far they'd traveled and the courage they'd shown along the way. And it touched something in her that these girls were set on getting home to their father. So once they'd been fed breakfast—a second one, in Lizzie's case; she had quite an appetite—Frau Moritz handed them clean pinnies and caps to wear.

"Hard workers are welcome here," the housekeeper said. "We'll have that sea crossing paid for in no time."

Agatha, who'd made a miraculous recovery, took a shine to both girls. At first Felix felt almost jealous at the sight of them giggling together as they worked. But the good thing was it kept Agatha off his back. Anyway, he had things to do, or rather, lies to tell. In helping Lizzie with her plan, he'd have to do quite a lot of both.

To Lord Byron, Felix complained of toothache and was promptly given a small bottle of laudanum for the pain. To Frau Moritz, he said he felt weak and could he please have today's serving of meat raw for strength. At suppertime, he admitted he still felt unwell and was sent to bed early. He felt almost guilty for the kindness he was shown. It took a lot of cunning to drug a wolf.

By nightfall it was done. The wolf lay snoring in its wooden crate out in the stable yard. Neither Mr. Shelley nor Lord Byron had cared to shoot it.

214

"Good grief, no," Mr. Shelley had said. "I don't eat animals, so why on earth would I kill one?" Lord Byron, who was known to be fond of animals, said the very thought of shooting such a beautiful beast had brought on a bilious attack. And Dr. Polidori, who came to tend his friend, insisted it was against his principles as a man of medicine to destroy a life. So someone else—a local farmer—was expected with his rifle in the morning.

Lizzie had wanted to borrow a horse, but in the end they settled on carrying the wolf between them. Up close, it smelled strongly of beast and outside places; Felix wondered if the smell would ever leave his hands, though Peg had no qualms. She insisted on stroking the wolf's head and talking to it as if it were an old friend.

"Time for us to go," Felix told Peg, easing her off the animal as they left the stable yard. "Your job's to lead the way. Follow the sheep track up the hill as far as it goes."

The wolf was a heavy, awkward thing to carry. Felix took its shoulders, its great head lolling from side to side at every step. Lizzie had the back end, and though she grunted under her breath, she kept up a good pace. They had to stop often, however, especially as the path got steeper, because of the rocks and loose soil underfoot.

It grew colder too. The night was clear and full of glittering stars. And soon they were high enough to hear frost crunching beneath their feet and feel the air burning their lungs.

"Is that the comet?" Peg asked, pointing to the sky.

Felix stopped. Shifting his grip on the wolf, he looked up. He didn't spot it straight away. The comet was little more than a smudge now, the other stars much bigger and brighter.

"Your strange star's leaving us, Lizzie," he said.

"Good," said Lizzie. "And so's this wolf soon, or I swear my arms will drop off."

They trudged on for another mile or so until they reached the pine forest. The grass was thinner here. Mostly it was stones and bare rock underfoot, and the odd patch of last winter's snow. Up ahead, out of sight, came the strange, eerie groaning of the glacier.

"This looks like a decent spot to release him," said Felix, stopping at the edge of the forest.

Gently, but very gladly, they laid the wolf on the ground. As they straightened up, Lizzie's fingertips briefly touched the animal's head. "Goodbye, poor creature. I hope wolves are kinder to you than us humans have been."

Peg tried to throw her arms around it and lay her cheek against its fur.

"He'll wake up soon, so we'd better keep back," Felix said, taking Peg's hand and gently pulling her away.

They crouched behind a rock a few yards off. An icy wind cut into Felix's skin. Beside him, Lizzie's teeth chattered with cold, but Peg sat still as stone, eyes fixed on the wolf.

The wolf woke suddenly. Jumping to its feet, it sniffed the air and sneezed. It staggered a little, then stretched, first its front legs, then each back one, pointing its toes like a dancer. Next there was more sniffing—of the ground, the nearby stand of trees and every boulder and blade of grass in between. Finally, the wolf stopped, threw back its head and howled.

The sound made Felix's skin prickle. If this was what Lizzie had heard coming from the stables at Eden Court, no wonder she'd been intrigued. It was such a sorrowful, heart-wrenching cry.

And then, the most marvelous thing.

216

From the forest, two dark shapes emerged.

"Wolves!" Peg breathed.

Felix felt something swell inside his chest.

These wild wolves padded right up to the newcomer. Sniffed him. Circled him. Bared their teeth. They were bigger than the captive wolf. One was pale-coated, with a torn right ear. The other was harder to see, owing to the darkness of its fur, though its eyes glinted bright blue in the moonlight. Their wolf wagged his tail in low, gentle sweeps. His ears went down and he cowered as if he was suddenly shy.

"He wants to be friends," whispered Peg. "It's like dogs in our village do when they like each other."

Sure enough, it wasn't long before the wolves became more playful. They mouthed each other's muzzles, lazily at first, as if they were testing things out. Then, growing in confidence, they pranced, shoulder to shoulder, in ever-widening circles. It was almost as if they knew they were being watched, Felix thought. When the game got too rough, the pale wolf nipped at hind legs. And their wolf would stop at once, fall to the ground and roll over. The others would stop too, panting, tails wagging.

It went on for quite a while, this wonderful display. Felix, arms hugging his knees, whispered what was happening in Lizzie's ear. He wanted her to live the moment with him.

Eventually, though, something caught the wolves' attention—an owl maybe, or deer in the woods. Ears pricked, they stood stock-still. Then their wolf rubbed his muzzle against the pale wolf's cheeks. And all three loped off together into the forest.

* * *

The next day when the Shelleys came to lunch, it was Felix's turn to serve.

"I hear the wolf escaped last night," Mr. Shelley said.

"Yes, sir, it did," Felix replied.

"I'm glad. It deserved to be free."

Heaping vegetables—but no meat—onto Mr. Shelley's plate, Felix had to agree. Yet it was hard to keep his mind on the job. Especially when, across the table, Lord Byron was speaking in a loud voice about him.

"So you think Felix has the makings of a great man, do you, Mary?"

"I do. You should take him with you back to London. He's wasted out here in the wilds."

Felix fought the urge to smile. He'd go to London at the drop of a hat; all Lord Byron had to do was ask. But the conversation quickly moved on.

"And your ghost story, Mary? Have you thought of one yet?"

Mary shot Felix a look.

"I believe I have," she said. "In fact, I'm going to start writing it today while it's still fresh in my mind."

As Felix met her gaze, an understanding passed between them.

Her story, he knew, would be all of theirs: his, Lizzie's, Peg's, even Mary's. It would weave and warn and speak of untold things.

And it would absolutely freeze the blood.

Epilogue

LONDON
JANUARY 1818

Chapter 30

TO FELIX'S AMAZEMENT, IT HAD snowed in the night. It wasn't deep, mountaintop snow or the strange red variety he'd once heard spoken of at Diodati. But it was lovely. For a moment, the rooftops of London and the noisy streets below looked as clean and unspoiled as fresh linen. He sighed heartily, and rather happily. Today was going to be a special day; it was as if the city itself agreed.

Excitement had got them up early.

"The cats won't go out in it, not even Spider," Peg said, standing on the back steps with the door wide open, snow-flakes and cats at her feet. "The parrot doesn't like it much either. Nor the otter."

"Then shut the blasted door. It's perishing cold," Lizzie replied. She sat as close to the fire as a person could get, toasting bread on a fork for breakfast. In the seat opposite, drinking tea, was Da. These days he quite enjoyed his daughters' bickering; he knew it came from a deep, fierce affection that nothing and no one would change.

Life, though, *had* changed, and it was amazing how quickly they'd all got used to it. Right at this moment, a bright green parrot swooped across the kitchen to perch on Lizzie's shoulder. To anyone else, it would've been a bizarre spectacle. Especially as by her feet a fox lay curled up asleep, and in her lap sat a rather plump hen. But to Felix and Peg and Lizzie and Da, it was as normal as normal could be.

The four of them had come to London a year ago. Lord Byron, in the end, didn't return to England. He went to Italy with Dr. Polidori in the hope of discouraging Miss Clairmont's persistent attentions. Before he left, he did offer Felix a position.

"My London house needs keeping an eye on in my absence," he said. "Also I've a few animals there—a rather exotic collection, as it happens. Find someone to tend them if you can."

Felix had packed his one small bag that very day. He took a boat to England, but instead of traveling down the Thames to London, he sought out a distant village called Sweepfield. It took two days to reach it on roads deep in mud. When finally he jumped stiff and sore from the cart, he was greeted only by stares.

"Well, he isn't from round here," a man said, looking Felix up and down.

"No, Mr. Henderson, he in't," said another. "And if he's come 'ere in search of Eden Court he'll be disappointed an' all."

Yet two people did show him kindness—a beautiful girl called Mercy, who offered him orange drops from a paper bag, and her sweetheart, Isaac Blake. They knew exactly where he'd find Lizzie and Peg, and took him there without delay.

Outside a moss-roofed cottage he stood in a yard teeming with young geese and broke his news.

"Would you come to London with me, Lizzie? And you, Peg?"

They'd blinked as if they didn't understand what he asked. Then a man, tall and dark and so very obviously their da, emerged from an outbuilding and demanded to know what all the fuss was about.

Felix felt a sudden panic. Lizzie, sleeves rolled up, a goose tucked under each arm, looked strong and well. Peg, swinging on her da's hand, was smiling. Less than half a mile away in the churchyard lay their own dear mother. He couldn't imagine how they'd ever bear to leave this place.

Yet Sweepfield wasn't just about family and geese and kind people like Mercy and Isaac. There was another, darker side—the Sweepfield that stared and gossiped and didn't like difference. He'd felt it himself earlier when he'd climbed down from the cart. Life here hadn't always been easy for the Applebys. And when Felix heard of Lizzie and Peg's final journey home to England, and how their da had been at Southampton docks to greet them, he knew this family wouldn't be split up again.

In the end, they didn't take much persuading. Da agreed to come to London, for since Eden Court had gone, so too had much of his work.

"Just for a while, to see what it's like," he'd said, though everyone knew the real reason was he couldn't bear to let his daughters out of his sight.

That had been last January. In a city expanding daily with new people and new buildings, Da's carpentry skills were much in demand. Meanwhile, Lizzie, like Felix, quickly grew to love London. There was so much life here. So much to experience. And she could walk out every day, blind and scarred, and know there'd always be something more thrilling for people to gawp at than her.

Today, for instance, there was a certain book being

published. It was called *Frankenstein; or, The Modern Prometheus*. Prometheus, Lizzie said, had stolen fire from the Greek gods.

"Is this book about Greek people, then?" Peg asked.

"No," said Lizzie, biting back a laugh. "It's about someone who tries too hard to be clever."

Mary hadn't put her name to the book. People would judge it wrongly, she said, if they thought a young woman was the author. She'd recently made an uneasy peace with her father, Mr. Godwin, who called himself a radical but was still rather old-fashioned where his daughter was concerned. She didn't want to upset him again. Yet already early reviews of *Frankenstein* were calling it "a depravity," which made Felix and Lizzie all the more intrigued. Together they'd saved up sixteen shillings. And today, they were going to walk to Mary's publisher in the East End to buy a copy.

Once toast had been eaten and the animals fed, they all set off into the cold. Byron's house—vast, cream-colored, absurdly expensive—sat on a busy Mayfair street. Under the wheels of countless carriages and hackney cabs, the snow had already turned to brown slush. Peg ran on ahead, plaits jiggling between her shoulders.

"Come straight home afterwards, won't you?" Da said as he left them at the top of the street for the place—a new cheese shop—where he was making counters and shelves.

"Yes, Da," Lizzie said. "Stop worrying. We'll be fine."

With Da gone, Felix relaxed a little.

"May I?" he asked, placing Lizzie's hand in the crook of his elbow.

She laughed and did a wobbly curtsey. "Why, thank you, kind sir."

First they went through Mayfair, past Hyde Park and then

down towards the river. It wasn't the quickest route, and normally the stink alone was enough to make you retch—never mind what you might spy floating in the water. Yet these past few days the frost had been very hard, so it was worth a look to see if the river had frozen over.

Near Covent Garden, the streets narrowed. It made everything seem busier and noisier. There were pie shops and gin shops, and down side alleys strewn with laundry, lodging houses shouted their wares. Everywhere you looked were peddlers selling face lotions or sheet music or hot fried herrings.

All the while, their sixteen shillings jingled in Lizzie's pocket. For safekeeping, she rested her hand on top in case of pickpockets. Her other hand stayed on Felix's arm, and it made him feel rather proud.

"How much further to the river?" Peg called over her shoulder.

Felix pointed up ahead. "It's at the end of the street. Watch where you're stepping, though."

These streets right near the river were often the worst. People got careless with their chamber pots, and today the cobbles were slippery and squelchy underfoot.

The river, when they reached it, wasn't frozen after all. It was, as usual, full of life. Ferry boats darted back and forth and barges glided upstream. Peg stuck out her bottom lip in disappointment.

"I hoped there'd be one of them frost fairs or something," she said.

"Never mind," Lizzie said. "Let's keep walking. It's too cold to stand still."

Felix liked the way her cheeks had gone pink. But she was right, it was bone-chillingly cold, and looking closely, he saw how the river seemed to be thickening up. Already ice was forming around jetties and near the bank.

"Reckon it won't be long before the river does freeze, Peg. Not if this cold keeps going," he said.

They followed the river as far as St. Paul's, then veered off through Spitalfields and into the East End.

"The address is Finsbury Square," Felix said.

He'd written it down on a scrap of paper, together with the publisher's name of Lackington and Hughes. In his head, he'd imagined a dark little shop where Mary could launch her book without fuss. Yet they found Lackington and Hughes on a busy street corner. It stood four stories high, with lavishly arched windows and a wide front door.

"Blimey!" Peg said, wiping her feet extra hard on the door-mat.

The book was on display at the counter. Against the other leather-bound, gilt-edged books, it looked small and rather plain. There weren't many copies for sale.

"Can I help you young people?" said a gentleman in a white curled wig.

"We'd like to purchase a copy of *Frankenstein*, please," Lizzie said.

The man's eyes twinkled in delight.

"Of course, of course! A work of genius, no less! Everyone will be reading it very soon!" And he began wrapping a copy in paper.

Funny, Felix thought, as he watched the man tie the package with string, to see a book in a shop and know the person who wrote it. To have been there at the start, when the idea began. Yet when Lizzie went to give the man their sixteen shillings, her pocket had indeed been picked.

"But I had the coins. Even as far as Covent Garden, I had them," she wailed.

The man raised his eyebrows and began unwrapping the book again.

"I'm sorry, miss," he said. "No money, no purchase."

Felix tried to keep his disappointment in check. Putting his arm through Lizzie's, he steered her back towards the door.

"'Tis such a shame," Lizzie said, close to tears.

Felix agreed. "Mary would've wanted us to read her book."

The bookseller must have overheard, for he called after them. "Young man! Did you just say Mary?"

"Yes," said Felix, turning round. "Mary Shelley, or Mary Godwin as was." For Mary and Percy were now properly married.

"Ah, well." The man's face brightened. "In that case . . ."

He beckoned them back to the counter.

"Mrs. Shelley told only a few very special people that this book was her work," the bookseller said. He rewrapped the package and handed it to Lizzie. "So you're right, she obviously *did* mean you to read it. How else could you have known?"

Back at home, they gathered round the fire. Lizzie and Peg huddled under blankets with various cats and dogs. The bright green parrot perched, as usual, on Lizzie's shoulder. Felix took the seat nearest the window, for it was his job to read out loud. And read he did, all that day and into the evening. He read the next day too. The story was so gripping he couldn't stop.

They heard of a scientist called Dr. Frankenstein, whose name bore a close resemblance to that of a certain lady with an interest in wolves. There was a young man called Felix, who had a sister called Agatha and a kind, blind father. One of the main characters was a girl called Elizabeth—Lizzie—and there was a young child who went missing, and even a servant with the surname Moritz.

But when, a long time later, Felix turned the final page, he knew there was more to this story than names. In it was a mother whose death broke her children's hearts. There were kind fathers, like Lizzie's, and ones like Mary's who were distant and cool.

There were people who, time and time again, judged others for how they looked.

This was his story. And Lizzie's. And Mary's. It was even Miss Stine's, in part.

For the book was also about ambition. About wanting to be the biggest, the best, the most famous at any cost. It was about pushing the boundaries of discovery. Most of all, though, it was a warning: without love and kindness, we all become monsters. Just like their captured wolf, which, Felix couldn't forget, had killed a man. Yet, given freedom and the company of its own kind, it had padded off across the snow, meek as a lamb.

In the end, Mary's story had been a tale to freeze the blood. Yet it was just that: a story. Felix could close its pages and look up. And there he'd see Lizzie and Peg, and he'd thank his good fortune. It made him glow like a star.

How *Frankenstein* Inspired *Strange Star*

History tells us much about the writing of *Frankenstein.* The year 1816 was known as "The Year Without Summer." The weather, unusually cold and wet with frequent thunderstorms, was the result of a huge volcanic eruption in Indonesia. Ash in the atmosphere altered the climate—and yes, there really were reports of red snow.

We know Mary Shelley stayed at the Villa Diodati in June 1816 with Percy Shelley, Lord Byron and Dr. John Polidori. There are also accounts of the Shelleys adopting a child whilst in Europe, though the arrangement mysteriously fell through. One night the friends challenged each other to tell ghost stories. Only Mary was stuck for something to write.

History then grows vague: Some accounts say Mary came up with the story for *Frankenstein* the very next day. Others say it was written much later, and was influenced by many things in her life: her own mother, who died giving birth to her; scientific advances of the time: society's prejudices towards women and people of color. And perhaps even the visit she made to a man named Andrew Crosse, who experimented with electricity at a house called Fyne Court in the Somerset hills.

Where the facts end, fiction begins. I had great fun filling in the gaps of what we know about Mary Shelley's world. There's no mention of the Villa Diodati in *Frankenstein*. There isn't a comet. No one gets struck by lightning—not directly—and I don't believe the book contains a single wolf.

Yet I've also tried to make my story echo Mary Shelley's in certain ways. Felix, Agatha, Elizabeth (Lizzie), Mr. Walton and Moritz are all names taken from *Frankenstein*. *Strange Star* is about scientific ambition: Miss Stine experiments with electricity regardless of the consequences, just as Victor Frankenstein does in Shelley's original. There is a blind character in *Frankenstein* who doesn't judge people by their appearance. Many of the characters in *Strange Star* face prejudice because of how they look or who they are.

For me, *Frankenstein* is a great story, and Mary Shelley an inspirational woman. I really hope reading *Strange Star* will make you want to discover more about both for yourself.

About the Author

Emma Carroll was a high school English teacher before leaving to write full-time. She has also worked as a reporter, an avocado picker, and the person who punches holes into Filofax paper. She recently graduated with distinction from Bath Spa University with an MA in Writing for Young People. She lives in the Somerset hills of England with her husband and two terriers. *Strange Star* is Emma's fourth novel. To learn more about Emma and her books, visit emmacarrollauthor.wordpress.com, follow @emmac2603 on Twitter, and also look for *In Darkling Wood*, available now from Delacorte Press.